SOUTH CAROLINA SLAVE NARRATIVES

A Folk History of Slavery in South Carolina
from Interviews with Former Slaves

* * *

Typewritten records prepared by
THE FEDERAL WRITERS' PROJECT
1936-1938

* * *

Published in cooperation with
THE LIBRARY OF CONGRESS

APPLEWOOD BOOKS
Bedford, Massachusetts

The LIBRARY
of CONGRESS

A portion of the proceeds from the sale
of this book is donated to the Library of
Congress, which holds the original Slave
Narratives in its collection.

Thank you for purchasing an Applewood book.
Applewood reprints America's lively classics
--books from the past that are still of
interest to modern readers. For a free copy
of our current catalog, write to:

Applewood Books
P.O. Box 365
Bedford, MA 01730

ISBN 1-55709-023-8

FOREWORD

More than 140 years have elapsed since the ratification of the Thirteenth Amendment to the U.S. Constitution declared slavery illegal in the United States, yet America is still wrestling with the legacy of slavery. One way to examine and understand the legacy of the 19th Century's "peculiar institution" in the 21st century is to read and listen to the stories of those who actually lived as slaves. It is through a close reading of these personal narratives that Americans can widen their understanding of the past, thus enriching the common memory we share.

The American Folklife Center at the Library of Congress is fortunate to hold a powerful and priceless sampling of sound recordings, manuscript interviews, and photographs of former slaves. The recordings of former slaves were made in the 1930s and early 1940s by folklorists John A. and Ruby T. Lomax, Alan Lomax, Zora Neale Hurston, Mary Elizabeth Barnicle, John Henry Faulk, Roscoe Lews, and others. These aural accounts provide the only existing sound of voices from the institution of slavery by individuals who had been held in bondage three generations earlier. These voices can be heard by visiting the web site http://memory.loc.gov/ammem/collections/voices/. Added to the Folklife Center collections, many of the narratives from manuscript sources, which you find in this volume, were collected under the auspices of the United States Works Progress Administration (WPA), and were known as the slave narrative collection. These transcripts are found in the Library of Congress Manuscript Division. Finally, in addition to the Folklife Center photographs, a treasure trove of Farm Security Administration (FSA) photographs (including those of many former slaves) reside in the Prints and Photographs Division here at the nation's library. Together, these primary source materials on audio tape, manuscript and photographic formats are a unique research collection for all who would wish to study and understand the emotions, nightmares, dreams, and determination of former slaves in the United States.

The slave narrative sound recordings, manuscript materials, and photographs are invaluable as windows through which we can observe and be touched by the experiences of slaves who lived in the mid-19th century. At the same time, these archival materials are the fruits of an extraordinary documentary effort of the 1930s. The federal government, as part of its response to the Great Depression, organized unprecedented national initiatives to document the lives, experiences, and cultural traditions of ordinary Americans. The slave narratives, as documents of the Federal Writers Project, established and delineated our modern concept of "oral history." Oral history, made possible by the advent of sound recording technology, was "invented" by folklorists, writers, and other cultural documentarians under the aegis of the Library of Congress and various WPA offices—especially the Federal Writers' project—during the 1930s. Oral history has subsequently become both a new tool for the discipline of history, and a new cultural pastime undertaken in homes, schools, and communities by Americans of all walks of life. The slave narratives you read in the pages that follow stand as our first national exploration of the idea of oral history, and the first time that ordinary Americans were made part of the historical record.

The American Folklife Center has expanded upon the WPA tradition by continuing to collect oral histories from ordinary Americans. Contemporary projects such as our Veterans History Project, StoryCorps Project, Voices of Civil Rights Project, as well as our work to capture the stories of Americans after September 11, 2001 and of the survivors of Hurricanes Katrina and Rita, are all adding to the Library of Congress holdings that will enrich the history books of the future. They are the oral histories of the 21st century.

Frederick Douglas once asked: can "the white and colored people of this country be blended into a common nationality, and enjoy together . . . under the same flag, the inestimable blessings of life, liberty, and the pursuit of happiness, as neighborly citizens of a common country? I believe they can." We hope that the words of the former slaves in these editions from Applewood Books will help Americans achieve Frederick Douglas's vision of America by enlarging our understanding of the legacy of slavery in all of our lives. At the same time, we in the American Folklife Center and the Library of Congress hope these books will help readers understand the importance of oral history in documenting American life and culture—giving a voice to all as we create our common history.

Peggy A. Bulger

Peggy Bulger
Director, The American Folklife Center
Library of Congress

A NOTE FROM THE PUBLISHER

Since 1976, Applewood Books has been republishing books from America's past. Our mission is to build a picture of America through its primary sources. The book you hold in your hand is a testament to that mission. Published in cooperation with the Library of Congress, this collection of slave narratives is reproduced exactly as writers in the Works Progress Administration's Federal Writers' Project (1936–1938) originally typed them.

As publishers, we thought about how to present these documents. Rather than making them more readable by resetting the type, we felt that there was more value in presenting the narratives in their original form. We believe that to fully understand any primary source, one must understand the period of time in which the source was written or recorded. Collected seventy years after the emancipation of American slaves, these narratives had been preserved by the Library of Congress, fortunately, as they were originally created. In 1941, the Library of Congress microfilmed the typewritten pages on which the narratives were originally recorded. In 2001, the Library of Congress digitized the microfilm and made the narratives available on their American Memory web site. From these pages we have reproduced the original documents, including both the marks of the writers of the time and the inconsistencies of the type. Some pages were missing or completely illegible, and we have used a simple typescript provided by the Library of Congress so that the page can be read. Although the font occasionally can make these narratives difficult to read, we believe that it is important not only to preserve the narratives of the slaves but also to preserve the documents themselves, thereby commemorating the groundbreaking effort that produced them. That way, also, we can give you, the reader, not only a collection of the life stories of ex-slaves, but also a glimpse into the time in which these stories were collected, the 1930s.

These are powerful stories by those who lived through slavery. No institution was more divisive in American history than slavery. From the very founding of America and to the present day, slavery has touched us all. We hope these real stories of real lives are preserved for generations of Americans to come.

INFORMANTS

FOLK LORE: FOLK TALES (Negro).

"Marse Glenn had 64 slaves. On Sat'day night, de darkies
would have a little fun on de side. A way off from de big house,
down in de pastur' dar wuz about de bigges' gully what I is ebber
seed. Dat wuz de place whar us collected mos' ev'ry Sa'day night fer
our lil' mite o' fun frum de white folks hearin'. Sometime it wuz
so dark dat you could not see de fingers on yo' han' when you would
raise it fo' your face. Dem wuz sho' scheechy nights; de shhreech-
iest what I is ever witnessed. in all o' my born natu'al days. Den
of cose, dar wuz de moon-light nights when a darky could see; den
he see too much. De pastur' wuz big and de trees made dark spots in
it on de brightest nights. All kind o' varmints tuck and hollered
at ye as ye being gwine along to reach dat gully. Cose us would go
in droves sometime, and den us would go alone to de gully sometime.
When us started together, look like us would git parted 'fo we
reach de gully all together. One of us see som'tin and take to runnin'. Maybe de other darkies in de drove, de wouldN't see nothin'
jas den. Dats zactly how it is wid de spirits. De mout (might) sho
de'self to you and not to me. De acts raal queer all de way round.
Dey can take a notion to scare de daylights outtin you when you is
wid a gang; or dey kin scare de whole gang; den, on de other hand,
dey kin sho de'self off to jes two or three. It ain't never no
knowin' as to how and when dem things is gwine to come in your
path right fo your very eyes; specially when you is partakin' in
some raal dark secret whar you is planned to act raal sof' and
quiet like all de way through.

"Dem things bees light on dark nights; de shines de'-
self jes like dese 'lectric lights does out dar in dat street
ever' night, 'cept dey is a scaird waary light dat dey shines wid.
On light nights, I is seed dem look, furs dark like a tree shad'er;
den dey gits raal scaary white. T'aint no use fer white folks to
low dat it ain't no haints, an' grievements dat follows ye all
around, kaise I is done had to many 'spriences wid dem. Den dare is
dese young niggers what ain't fit to be called darkies, dat tries to
ac' eddicated, and says dat it ain't any spe'rits dat walks de
earth. When dey lows dat to me, I rolls my old eyes at dem an'
axes dem how comes dey runs so fas' through de woods at night. Yes
sirree, dem fool niggers sees dem jes as I does. Raaly de white
folks doesn't have eyes fer sech as we darkies does; but dey bees
dare jes de same.

" Never mindin' all o' dat, we n'used to steal our hog
ev'er sa'day night and take off to de gully whar us'd git him
dressed and barbecued. Niggers has de mos'es fun at a barbecue dat
dare is to be had. As none o' our gang didn't have no 'ligion, us
never felt no scruples bout not gettin de 'cue' ready fo' Sunday.
Us'd git back to de big house along in de evenin' o' Sunday. Den
Marse, he come out in de yard an' low whar wuz you niggers dis
mornin'. How come de chilluns had to do de work round here. Us
would tell some lie bout gwine to a church 'siety meetin'. But we
got raal scairt and mose 'cided dat de best plan wuz to do away wid
de barbecue in de holler. Conjin 'Doc.' say dat he done put a spell
on ole Marse so dat he wuz 'blevin ev'y think dat us tole him bout
Sa'day night and Sunday morning. Dat give our minds 'lief; but it
turned out dat in a few weeks de Marse come out from under de spell.

Doc never even knowed nothin' bout it. Marse had done got to
countin' his hogs ever' week. When he cotch us, us wuz all punished
wid a hard long task. Dat cured me o' believing in any conjuring
an' charmin' but I still kno's dat dare is haints; kaise ever time
you goes to dat gully at night, up to dis very day, you ken hear
hogs still gruntin' in it, but you can't see nothing.

"After Marse Glenn tuck and died, all o' de white folks
went off and lef' de plantation. Some mo' folks dat wuz not o'
quality, come to live dare an' run de plantation. It wuz done freedom den. Wo'nt long fo dem folks pull up and lef' raal onexpected
like. I doesn't recollect what dey went by , fat is done slipped
my mind; but I must 'am knowed. But dey lowed dat de house wuz to
draffy and dat dey couldn't keep de smoke in de chimney an' dat
de doo's would not stay shet. Also dey lowed dat folks prowled
aroun' in de yard in de night time a keepin' dem awake.

"Den Marse Gleen's boys put Mammy in de house to keep it
fer'em. But Lawd God! Mammy said dat de furs night she stayed dare
de haints nebber let her git not narr'y mite o' sleep. Us all had
lowed dat wuz de raal reason dem white folks lef out so fas'. When
Mammy could not live in dat big house whar she had stayed fer years,
it won't no use fer nobody else to try. Mammy low dat it de Marse
a lookin' fer his money what he done tuck and burried and de boys
couldn't find no sign o' it. Atter dat, de sons tuck an' tacked a
sign on de front gate, offering $200.00 to de man, white or black,
dat would stay dar and fin' out whar dat money wuz bur'ried. Our
preacher, the Rev. Wallace, lowed dat he would stay dat and find
out whar dat money wuz from de spirits. He knowed dat dey wuz tryin
to sho de spot what dat money wuz.

"He went to bed. A dog began running down dem steps; and a black cat run across de room dat turned to white befo' it run into de wall. Den a pair of white horses come down de stairway a rattling chains fer harness. Next a woman dressed in white come in dat room. Brother Wallace up and lit out dat house and he never went back no mo'.

" Another preacher tried stayin' dar. He said he gwine to keep his head kivered plum up. Some'tin unkivered it and he seed a white goat a grinnin' at him. But as he wuz a brave man and trus' de Lawd, he lowed, 'What you want wid me nohow?' The goat said,'what is you doin' here. Raise, I knows dat you ain't sleep.' De preacher say, 'I wants you to tell me what ole Marse don tuck and hid dat money?' De goat grin and low, 'How come you don' look under your pillar, sometime?' Den he run away. De preacher hopped up and looked under de pillar, and dar wuz de money sho nuf. Peers like it wuz de one on de lef' end o' de back porch, but I jes remembers 'bout dat."

SOURCE: Mrs. M.E. Abrams, Whitmire, S.C.; told her by old "uncle" "Mad" Griffin, Whitmire, (Col. 82 yrs.) Interviewer: Caldwell Sims, Union, S.C. 2/25/37.

REFLECTIONS OF EZRA ADAMS

EX-SLAVE 83 YEARS OLD

Ezra Adams is incapable of self-support, owing to ill health. He is very well taken care of by a niece, who lives on the Caughman land just off S. C. #6, and near Swansea, S. C.

"My mammy and pappy b'long to Marster Lawrence Adams, who had a big plantation in de eastern part of Lancaster County. He died four years after de Civil War and is buried right dere on de old plantation, in de Adams family burying grounds. I was de oldest of de five chillun in our family. I 'members I was a right smart size plow boy, when freedom come. I think I must of been 'bout ten or eleven years old, then. Dere's one thing I does know; de Yankees didn't tech our plantation, when they come through South Carolina. Up in de northern part of de county they sho' did destroy most all what folks had.

"You ain't gwine to believe dat de slaves on our plantation didn't stop workin' for old marster, even when they was told dat they was free. Us didn't want no more freedom than us was gittin' on our plantation already. Us knowed too well dat us was well took care of, wid a plenty of vittles to eat and tight log and board houses to live in. De slaves, where I lived, knowed after de war dat they had abundance of dat somethin' called freedom, what they could not eat, wear, and sleep in. Yes, sir, they soon found out dat freedom ain't nothin', 'less you is got somethin' to live on and a place to call home. Dis livin' on liberty is lak young folks livin' on love after they gits married. It just don't work. No, sir, it las' so long and not a bit longer. Don't tell me! It sho' don't hold good when you has to work, or when you gits hongry. You knows dat poor white folks and niggers has got to work to live, regardless of liberty, love, and all them things. I believes a person loves more better, when they feels

good. I knows from experience dat poor folks feels better when they has food

in deir frame and a few dimes to jingle in deir pockets. I knows what it means

to be a nigger, wid nothin'. Many times I had to turn every way I knowed to git

a bite to eat. I didn't care much 'bout clothes. What I needed in sich times

was food to keep my blood warm and gwine 'long.

"Boss, I don't want to think, and I knows I ain't gwine to say, a word,

not a word of evil against deir dust lyin' over yonder in deir graves. I was

old enough to know what de passin' 'way of old marster and missus meant to me. De

very stream of lifeblood in me was dryin' up, it 'peared lak. When marster died,

dat was my fust real sorrow. Three years later, missus passed 'way, dat was de time

of my second sorrow. Then, I 'minded myself of a little tree out dere in de woods

in November. Wid every sharp and cold wind of trouble dat blowed, more leaves of

dat tree turnt loose and went to de ground, just lak they was tryin' to follow her.

It seem lak, when she was gone, I was just lak dat tree wid all de leaves gone,

naked and friendless. It took me a long time to git over all dat; same way wid

de little tree, it had to pass through winter and wait on spring to see life again.

"I has farmed 'most all my life and, if I was not so old, I would be doin'

dat same thing now. If a poor man wants to enjoy a little freedom, let him go on

de farm and work for hisself. It is sho' worth somethin' to be boss, and, on de

farm you can be boss all you want to, 'less de man 'low his wife to hold dat 'port-

ant post. A man wid a good wife, one dat pulls wid him, can see and feel some

pleasure and experience some independence. But, bless your soul, if he gits a

woman what wants to be both husband and wife, fare-you-well and goodbye, too, to

all love, pleasure, and independence; 'cause you sho' is gwine to ketch hell here

and no mild climate whenever you goes 'way. A bad man is worse, but a bad woman is almost terrible.

"White man, dere is too many peoples in dese big towns and cities. Dere is more of them than dere is jobs to make a livin' wid. When some of them find out dat they can't make a livin', they turns to mischief, de easy way they thinks, takin' widout pay or work, dat which b'longs to other people. If I understands right, de fust sin dat was committed in de world was de takin' of somethin' dat didn't b'long to de one what took it. De gentleman what done dis was dat man Adam, back yonder in de garden. If what Adam done back yonder would happen now, he would be guilty of crime. Dat's how 'ciety names sin. Well, what I got to say is dis: If de courts, now, would give out justice and punishment as quick as dat what de Good Master give to Adam, dere would be less crime in de land I believes. But I 'spose de courts would be better if they had de same jurisdiction as de Master has. Yes, sir, they would be gwine some then.

"I tells you, dis gittin' what don't b'long to you is de main cause of dese wars and troubles 'bout over dis world now. I hears de white folks say dat them Japanese is doin' dis very thing today in fightin' them Chinamens. Japan say dat China has done a terrible crime against them and de rest of de world, when it ain't nothin' but dat they wants somethin' what don't belong to them, and dat somethin' is to git more country. I may be wrong, anyhow, dat is what I has heard.

"What does I think de colored people need most? If you please sir, I want to say dis. I ain't got much learnin', 'cause dere was no schools hardly 'round where I was brung up, but I thinks dat good teachers and work is what de colored race needs worser than anything else. If they has learnin', they will be more ashame to commit crime, most of them will be; and, if they has work to do, they ain't gwine to have time to do so much wrong. Course dere is gwine to be black sheeps in most flocks, and it is gwine to take patience to git them out, but they will come out, just as sho' as you is born.

"Is de colored people superstitious? Listen at dat. You makes me laugh. All dat foolishness fust started wid de black man. De reason they is superstitious comes from nothin' but stompedown ignorance. De white chillun has been nursed by colored women and they has told them stories 'bout hants and sich lak. So de white chillun has growed up believin' some of dat stuff 'til they natchally pass it on from generation to generation. Here we is, both white and colored, still believin' some of them lies started back when de whites fust come to have de blacks 'round them.

"If you wants to know what I thinks is de best vittles, I's gwine to be obliged to omit (admit) dat it is cabbage sprouts in de spring, and it is collard greens after frost has struck them. After de best vittles, dere come some more what is mighty tasty, and they is hoghead and chittlings wid 'tatoes and turnips. Did you see dat? Here I is talkin' 'bout de joys of de appetite and water drapping from my mouth. I sho' must be gittin' hongry. I lak to eat. I has been a good eater all my life, but now I is gittin' so old dat 'cordin' to de scriptures, 'De grinders cease 'cause they are few', and too, 'Those dat look out de windows be darkened'. My old eyes and teeth is 'bout gone, and if they does go soon, they ain't gwine to beat dis old frame long, 'cause I is gwine to soon follow, I feels. I hope when I does go, I can be able to say what dat great General Stonewall Jackson say when he got kilt in de Civil War, 'I is gwine to cross de river and rest under de shade of de trees'."

Ezra Adams, Swansea (about 10 m. south of Columbia).

Project 1885 - 1.
Folk Lore
District No. 4.
May 27, 1937.

390088

Edited by:
J. J. Murray.

9

EX-SLAVE STORIES

"Aunt" Mary Adams was swinging easily back and forth in the porch swing as the writer stopped to speak to her. When questioned, she replied that she and her mother were ex-slaves and had belonged to Dr. C. E. Fleming. She was born in Columbia, but they were moved to Glenn Springs where her mother cooked for Dr. Fleming.

She remembers going with a white woman whose husband was in jail, to carry him something to eat. She said that Mr. Jim Milster was in that jail, but he lived to get out, and later kept a tin shop in Spartanburg.

"Yes sir, Dr. Fleming always kept enough for us Niggers to eat during the war. He was good to us. You know he married Miss Dean. Do you know Mrs. Lyles, Mrs. Simpson, Mr. Ed Fleming? Well, dey are my chilluns.

"Some man here told me one day that I was ninety years old, but I do not believe I am quite that old. I don't know how old I am, but I was walking during slavery times. I can't work now, for my feet hurt me and my fingers ain't straight."

She said all of her children were dead but two, that she knew of. She said that she had a room in that house and whiteb people gave her different things. As the writer told her good-bye, she said, "Good-bye, and may the Lord bless you".

SOURCE: "Aunt" Mary Adams, 363 S. Liberty Street, Spartanburg, S.C.
    Interviewer: F. S. DuPre, Spartanburg, S. C.

VICTORIA ADAMS

EX-SLAVE 90 YEARS OLD.

"You ask me to tell you something 'bout myself and de slaves in slavery times? Well Missy, I was borned a slave, nigh on to ninety years ago, right down here at Cedar Creek, in Fairfield County.

"My massa's name was Samuel Black and missus was named Martha. She used to be Martha Kirkland befo' she married. There was five chillun in de family; they was: Alice, Manning, Sally, Kirkland, and de baby, Eugene. De white folks live in a great big house up on a hill; it was right pretty, too.

"You wants to know how large de plantation was I lived on? Well, I don't know 'zackly but it was mighty large. There was forty of us slaves in all and it took all of us to keep de plantation goin'. De most of de niggers work in de field. They went to work as soon as it git light enough to see how to git 'round; then when twelve o'clock come, they all stops for dinner and don't go back to work 'til two. All of them work on 'til it git almost dark. No ma'am, they ain't do much work at night after they gits home.

"Massa Samuel ain't had no overseer, he look after his own plantation. My old granddaddy help him a whole heap though. He was a good nigger and massa trust him.

"After de crops was all gathered, de slaves still had plenty of work to do. I stayed in de house wid de white folks. De most I had to do was to keep de house clean up and nurse de chillun. I had a heap of pretty clothes to wear, 'cause my missus give me de old clothes and shoes dat Missy Sally throw 'way.

"De massa and missus was good to me but sometime I was so bad

they had to whip me. I 'members she used to whip me every time she
tell me to do something and I take too long to move 'long and do it.
One time my missus went off on a visit and left me at home. When she
come back, Sally told her that I put on a pair of Bubber's pants and
scrub de floor wid them on. Missus told me it was a sin for me to put
on a man's pants, and she whip me pretty bad. She say it's in de Bible
dat: 'A man shall not put on a woman's clothes, nor a woman put on a
man's clothes'. I ain't never see that in de Bible though, but from then
'til now, I ain't put on no more pants.

"De grown-up slaves was punished sometime too. When they didn't
feel like taking a whippin' they went off in de woods and stay 'til massa's
hounds track them down; then they'd bring them out and whip them. They
might as well not run away. Some of them never come back a-tall, don't
know what become of them. We ain't had no jail for slaves; never ain't see
none in chains neither. There was a guard-house right in de town but us
niggers never was carried to it. You ask me if I ever see a slave auction-
ed off? Yes ma'am, one time. I see a little girl 'bout ten years old sold
to a soldier man. Dis soldier man was married and didn't had no chillun
and he buy dis little girl to be company for his wife and to help her wid
de house work.

"White folks never teach us to read nor write much. They learned us our A, B, C's, and teach us to read some in de testament. De reason
they wouldn't teach us to read and white, was 'cause they was afraid de
slaves would write their own pass and go over to a free county. One old
nigger did learn enough to write his pass and got 'way wid it and went up
North.

"Missus Martha sho' did look after de slaves good when they was sick. Us had medicine made from herbs, leaves and roots; some of them was cat-nip, garlic root, tansy, and roots of burdock. De roots of burdock soaked in whiskey was mighty good medicine. We dipped asafetida in turpentine and hung it 'round our necks to keep off disease.

"Befo' de Yankees come thru, our peoples had let loose a lot of our hosses and de hosses strayed over to de Yankee side, and de Yankee men rode de hosses back over to our plantation. De Yankees asked us if we want to be free. I never say I did; I tell them I want to stay wid my missus and they went on and let me alone. They 'stroyed most everything we had 'cept a little vittles; took all de stock and take them wid them. They burned all de buildings 'cept de one de massa and missus was livin' in.

"It wasn't long after de Yankees went thru dat our missus told us dat we don't b'long to her and de massa no more. None of us left dat season. I got married de next year and left her. I like being free more better. Any niggers what like slavery time better, is lazy people dat don't want to do nothing.

"I married Fredrick Adams; he used to b'long to Miss Teeny Graddick but after he was freed he had to take another name. Mr. Jess Adams, a good fiddler dat my husband like to hang 'round, told him he could take his name if he wanted to and dats how he got de name of Adams. Us had four chillun; only one livin', dat Lula. She married John Entzminger and got several chillun. My gran'chillun a heap of comfort to me."

Home Address:
Colonial Heights,
Columbia, S. C.

FRANK ADAMSON
EX-SLAVE 82 YEARS OLD.

"I 'members when you was barefoot at de bottom; now I see you a settin' dere, gittin' bare at de top, as bare as de palm of my hand.

"I's been 'possum huntin' wid your pappy, when he lived on de Wateree, just after de war. One night us got into tribulation, I tells you! 'Twas 'bout midnight when de dogs make a tree. Your pappy climb up de tree, git 'bout halfway up, heard sumpin' dat once you hears it you never forgits, and dats de rattlin' of de rattles on a rattle snake's tail. Us both 'stinctly hear dat sound! What us do? Me on de ground, him up de tree, but where de snake? Dat was de misery, us didn't know. Dat snake give us fair warnin' though! Marster Sam (dats your pa) 'low: 'Frank, ease down on de ground! I'll just stay up here for a while.' I lay on them leaves, skeered to make a russle. Your pa up de tree skeered to go up or down! Broad daylight didn't move us. Sun come up, he look all 'round from his vantage up de tree, then come down, not 'til then, do I gits on my foots.

"Then I laugh and laugh and laugh, and ask Marster Sam how he felt. Marster Sam kinda frown and say: 'Damn I feels like hell! Git up dat tree! Don't you see dat 'possum up dere?' I say: 'But where de snake, Marster?' He say: 'Dat rattler done gone home, where me and you and dat 'possum gonna be pretty soon!'

"I b'longs to de Peays. De father of them all was, Kershaw Peay. My marster was his son, Nicholas; he was a fine man to just look at. My mistress was always tellin' him 'bout how fine and handsome-like he was. He must of got use to it; howsomever, marster grin every time she talk like dat.

"My pappy was bought from de Adamson peoples; they say they got him off de ship from Africa. He sho' was a man; he run all de other niggers 'way from my mammy and took up wid her widout askin' de marster. Her name was Lavinia. When us got free, he 'sisted on Adamson was de name us would go by. He name was William Adamson. Yes sir! my brothers was: Justus, Hillyard, and Donald, and my sisters was, Martha and Lizzettie.

"'Deed I did work befo' freedom. What I do? Hoed cotton, pick cotton, 'tend to calves and slop de pigs, under de 'vision of de overseer. Who he was? First one name Mr. Cary, he a good man. Another one Mr. Tim Gladden, burn you up whenever he just take a notion to pop his whip. Us boys run 'round in our shirt tails. He lak to see if he could lift de shirt tail widout techin' de skin. Just as often as not, though, he tech de skin. Little boy holler and Marster Tim laugh.

"Us live in quarters. Our beds was nailed to de sides of de house. Most of de chillun slept on pallets on de floor. Got water from a big spring.

"De white folks 'tend to you all right. Us had two doctors, Doctor Carlisle and Doctor James.

"I see some money, but never own any then. Had plenty to eat: Meat, bread, milk, lye hominy, horse apples, turnips, collards, pumpkins, and dat kind of truck.

"Was marster rich? How come he wasn't? He brag his land was ten miles square and he had a thousand slaves. Them poor white folks looked up to him lak God Almighty; they sho' did. They would have stuck their hands in de fire if he had of asked them to do it. He had a fish pond on top of de house and terraces wid strawberries, all over de place.

See them big rock columns down dere now? Dats all dats left of his
grandness and greatness. They done move de whippin' post dat was in
de backyard. Yes sah, it was a 'cessity wid them niggers. It stood
up and out to 'mind them dat if they didn't please de master and de
overseer, they'd hug dat post, and de lend of dat whip lash gwine to
flip to de hide of dat back of their's.

"I ain't a complainin'. He was a good master, bestest in de
land, but he just have to have a whippin' post, 'cause you'll find a
whole passle of bad niggers when you gits a thousand of them in one
flock.

"Screech owl holler? Women and men turn socks and stockings
wrong side out quick, dat they did, do it now, myself. I's black as
a crow but I's got a white folks heart. Didn't ketch me foolin' 'round
wid niggers in radical times. I's as close to white folks then as peas
in a pod. Wore de red shirt and drunk a heap of brandy in Columbia, dat
time us went down to General Hampton into power. I 'clare I hollered so
loud goin' 'long in de procession, dat a nice white lady run out one of
de houses down dere in Columbia, give me two biscuits and a drum stick
of chicken, patted me on de shoulder, and say: 'Thank God for all de
big black men dat can holler for Governor Hampton as loud as dis one
does.' Then I hollers some more for to please dat lady, though I had
to take de half chawed chicken out dis old mouth, and she laugh 'bout
dat 'til she cried. She did!

"Well, I'll be rockin' 'long balance of dese days, a hollerin'
for Mr. Roosevelt, just as loud as I holler then for Hampton.

"My young marsters was: Austin, Tom, and Nicholas; they was all right 'cept they tease you too hard maybe some time, and want to mix in wid de 'fairs of slave 'musements.

"Now what make you ask dat? Did me ever do any courtin'? You knows I did. Every he thing from a he king down to a bunty rooster gits 'cited 'bout she things. I's lay wake many nights 'bout sich things. It's de nature of a he, to take after de she. They do say dat a he angel ain't got dis to worry 'bout.

"I fust courted Martha Harrison. Us marry and jine de church. Us had nine chillun; seven of them livin'. A woman can't stand havin' chillun, lak a man. Carryin', sucklin', and 'tending to them wore her down, dat, wid de malaria of de Wateree brung her to her grave.

"I sorrow over her for weeks, maybe five months, then I got to thinking how I'd pair up wid dis one and dat one and de other one. Took to shavin' again and gwine to Winnsboro every Saturday, and different churches every Sunday. I hear a voice from de choir, one Sunday, dat makes me sit up and take notice of de gal on de off side in front. Well sir! a spasm of fright fust hit me dat I might not git her, dat I was too old for de likes of her, and dat some no 'count nigger might be in de way. In a few minutes I come to myself. I rise right up, walked into dat choir, stand by her side, and wid dis voice of mine, dat always 'tracts 'tention, jined in de hymn and out sung them all. It was easy from dat time on.

"I marry Kate at de close of dat revival. De day after de weddin', what you reckon? Don't know? Well, after gittin' breakfas' she went to de field, poke 'round her neck, basket on her head and picked two hundred pounds of cotton. Dats de kind of woman she is."

Project 1885-1
FOLKLORE
Spartanburg Dist 4
June 10, 1937

390117 V 4

Edited by:
Elmer Turnage 17

STORIES FROM EX-SLAVES

"I was born in Newberry County, S.C., near Belfast, about 1854. I was a slave of John Wallace. I was the only child, and when a small child, my mother was sold to Joe Liggins by my old master, Bob Adams. It is said that the old brick house where the Wallaces lived was built by a Eichleberger, but Dr. John Simpson lived there and sold it to Mr. Wallace. In the attic was an old skeleton which the children thought bewitched the house. None of them would go upstairs by themselves. I suppose old Dr. Simpson left it there. Sometimes later, it was taken out and buried. Marse Wallace had many slaves and kept them working, but he was not a strict master.

"I married Allen Andrews after the war. He went to the war with his master. He was at Columbia with the Confederate troops when Sherman burnt the place. Some of them, my husband included, was captured and taken to Richmond Va. They escaped and walked back home, but all but five or six fell out or died.

"My young master, Editor Bill Wallace, a son of Marse John, was a soldier. When he was sick at home, I fanned the flies from him with a home-made fan of peacock feathers, sewed to a long cane.

"After the war, the 'bush-whackers', called Ku Klux, rode there. Preacher Pitts' brother was one. They went to negro houses and killed the people. They wore caps over the head and eyes, but no long white gowns. An old muster ground was above there about three miles, near what is now Wadsworth School."

Source: Frances Andrews (col. 83), Newberry, S.C.
    Interviewer: G. Leland Summer, Newberry, S.C.

Project 1885-1
FOLKLORE
Spartanburg Dist.4
Sept. 22, 1937

390241 V.4

Edited by:
Elmer Turnage 18

STORIES FROM EX-SLAVES

"I live in a comfortable two-room cottage, which my son owns.
I can't do much work except a little washing and ironing. My grandchildren live with me. My other children help me a little when I
need it. I heard about the 40 acres of land and a mule the ex-
slaves would get after the war, but I didn't pay any attention to it.
They never got anything. I think this was put out by the Yankees
who didn't care about much 'cept getting money for themselves.

"I come from the Indian Creek section of Newberry County.
After about 1880 when things got natural, some of the slaves from
this section rented small one-horse farms and made their own money
and living. Some would rent small tracts of land on shares, giving
the landlord one-half the crop for use of the land.

"Everything is changed so much. I never learned to read
and write and all I know is what I heard in old times. But I think
the younger generation of negroes is different from what they used
to be. They go where they want to and do what they want to and don't
pay much attention to old folks anymore.

"My mother's mother come from Virginia and my mother's
father was born and raised in this county. I don't remember anything
about the Nat Turner Rebellion, and never heard anything about it.
We never had any slave up-risings in our neighborhood."

Source: Frances Andrews (83), Newberry, S.C.
        Interviewer: G.L. Summer, Newberry, S.C. 8/11/37.

Project 1885-(1)
Folklore
Spartanburg, S.C.
District No. 4
May 27, 1937.

Edited by
R.V. Williams

19

Lambright

Folk Lore: Folk Tales (negro)

"I was 'bout nine year ole when de big war broke
loose. My pa and ma 'longed to de Scotts what libbed in
Jonesville Township. When I got big 'nough to work, I was
gib to de youngest Scott boy. Soon atter dis, Sherman come
through Union County. No ma'm, I nebber seed Sherman but I
seed some of his soldiers. Dat's de time I run off in de wood
and not narry a soul knowed whar I was till de dus' had done
settled in de big road.

"Every Sunday, Marse Scott sent us to church in one
of his waggins. White folks rid to church in de buggy and Marse
went on de big saddle hoss. 'Bout dis time, Marse Scott went
to Columbia to git coffee and sugar. He stay mos' two weeks,
kaize he drive two fine hosses to de buggy 'long wid a long hind
end to fetch things to and fro in. De roads was real muddy and
de hosses haf to res' ever night. Den in Columbia, he would
have a little 'joyment befo' he come back home."

SOURCE: Miss Dorothy Lambright, W. Main St., Union, S.C. (Story
          told her by "Uncle Peter" Arthur. Information by
          Caldwell Sims, Union, S.C.

Code No.
Project, 1885-(1)
Prepared by Annie Ruth Davis
Place, Marion, S.C.
Date, January 4, 1938

No. Words_____
Reduced from___words
Rewritten by

JOSEPHINE BACCHUS
Ex-Slave, 75-80 Years   390418

"No, my mercy God, I don' know not one thought to speak
to you bout. Seems like, I does know your face, but I been
so sick all de year dat I can' hardly remember nothin. Yes,
sweetheart, I sho caught on to what you want. Oh, I wishes
I did know somethin bout dat old time war cause I tell you,
if I been know anything, I would sho pour it out to you. I
got burn out here de other day en I ain' got near a thing
left me, but a pair of stockings en dat old coat dere on de
bed. Dat how-come I stayin here wid Miss Celia. My husband,
he dead en she took me in over here for de present. No'um,
I haven't never had a nine months child. Reckon dat what
ailin me now. Bein dat I never had no mother to care for
me en give me a good attention like, I caught so much of
cold dat I ain' never been safe in de family way. Yes,mam,
I had my leg broke plenty times, but I ain' never been able
to jump de time. Lord, I got a misery in my back dere. I
hope it ain' de pneumonias."

"Well, you see, I couldn' tell you nothin bout my mother
cause I never didn' know nothin bout my mother. My Jesus, my
brother tell bout when dey had my mother layin out on de coolin
board, I went in de room whe' she was en axed her for somethin
to eat en pushed her head dat way. You know, I wouldn' touch
my hand to do nothin like dat, but I never know. Dat it, de

Code No.
Project, 1885-(1)
Prepared by Annie Ruth Davis
Place, Marion, S.C.
Date, January 4, 1938

No. Words_____
Reduced from___words
Rewritten by

Page 2.   21

coolin board, dat what dey used to have to lay all de dead
people on, but dis day en time, de undertaker takes dem en
fixes dem up right nice, I say. I tellin you, I ain' had
no sense since I lost my people. Sometimes, I axes de Lord
what he keepin me here for anyhow. Yes,mam, dat does come
to me often times in de night. Oh, it don' look like I gwine
ever get no better in dis life en if I don', I just prays to
God to be saved. Yes, Lord, I prays to be lifted to a restful
home."

"Just like as I been hear talk, some of de people fare
good in slavery time en some of dem fare rough. Dat been
accordin to de kind of task boss dey come up under. Now de
poor colored people in slavery time, dey give dem very little
rest en would whip some of dem most to death. Wouldn' none
of dem daresen to go from one plantation to another widout
dey had a furlough from dey boss. Yes,mam, if dey been catch
you comin back widout dat walkin paper de boss had give you,
great Jeruseleum, you would sho catch de devil next mornin.
My blessed a mercy, hear talk dey spill de poor nigger's
blood awful much in slavery time. Hear heap of dem was free
long time fore dey been know it cause de white folks, dey wanted to keep dem in bondage. Oh, my Lord, dey would cut dem so
hard till dey just slash de flesh right off dem. Yes,mam, dey
call dat thing dey been whip dem wid de cat o' nine tail. No,
darlin, I hear talk it been made out of pretty leather plaited

Code No.
Project, 1885-(1)
Prepared by Annie Ruth Davis
Place, Marion, S.C.
Date, January 4, 1938

No. Words_____
Reduced from____words
Rewritten by
_____
Page 3.   ₼ 22

most all de way en den all dat part down to de bottom, dey just left it loose to do de cuttin wid. Yes, honey, dem kind of whips was made out of pretty leather like one of dese horse whips. Yes,mam, dat been how it was in slavery time."

"Yankees! Oh, I hear folks speak bout de Yankees plunderin through de country plenty times. Hear bout de Yankees gwine all bout stealin white people silver. Say, everywhe' dey went en found white folks wid silver, dey would just clean de place up. Dat de blessed truth, too, cause dat exactly what I hear bout dem."

"Lord, pray Jesus, de white people sho been mighty proud to see dey niggers spreadin out in dem days, so dey tell me. Yes,mam, dey was glad to have a heap of colored people bout dem cause white folks couldn' work den no more den dey can work dese days like de colored people can. Reckon dey love to have dey niggers back yonder just like dey loves to have dem dese days to do what dey ain' been cut out to do. You see, dey would have two or three women on de plantation dat was good breeders en dey would have chillun pretty regular fore freedom come here. You know, some people does be right fast in catchin chillun. Yes'um, dey must been bless wid a pile of dem, I say, en every colored person used to follow up de same name as dey white folks been hear to."

Code No.
Project, 1885-(1)
Prepared by Annie Ruth Davis
Place, Marion, S.C.
Date, January 4, 1938

No. Words_____
Reduced from____words
Rewritten by_____

Page 4.

28

"No'um, I never didn' go to none of dem cornshuckin en
fodder pullin en all dem kind of thing. Reckon while dey
was at de cornshuckin, I must been somewhe' huntin somethin
to eat. Den dem kind of task was left to de men folks de
most of de time cause it been so hot, dey/force to strip to
do dat sort of a job."

"Lord, I sho remembers dat earth shake good as anything.
When it come on me, I was settin down wid my foots in a tub
of water. Yes, my Lord, I been had a age on me in de shake.
I remember, dere been such a shakin dat evenin, it made all
de people feel mighty queer like. It just come in a tremble
en first thing I know, I felt de difference in de crack of de
house. I run to my sister Jessie cause she had been live in
New York en she was well acquainted wid dat kind of gwine on.
She say, 'Josie, dis ain' nothin but dem shake I been tellin
you bout, but dis de first time it come here en you better be
a prayin.' En, honey, everything white en colored was emptied
out of doors dat night. Lord, dey was scared. Great Jeruseleum!
De people was scared everywhe'. Didn' nobody know what to make
of it. I tellin you, I betcha I was 30 years old in de shake."

"Now, I guess time you get done gettin up all dem memo-
randums, you gwine have a pile. I tell you, if you keep on,
you sho gwine have a bale cause dere a lot of slavery people
is spring up till now. I ought to could fetch back more to
speak to you bout, but just like I been tell you, I wasn' never

Code No.
Project, 1885-(1)
Prepared by Annie Ruth Davis
Place, Marion, S.C.
Date, January 4, 1938

No. Words_____
Reduced from____words
Rewritten by

Page 5.   ‥   24

cared for by a mother en I is caught on to a heap of rough-
ness just on account dat I ain' never had a mother to have
a care for me."

"Oh, de people never didn' put much faith to de doctors
in dem days. Mostly, dey would use de herbs in de fields
for dey medicine. Dere two herbs, I hear talk of. Dey was
black snake root en Sampson snake root. Say, if a person
never had a good appetite, dey would boil some of dat stuff
en mix it wid a little whiskey en rock candy en dat would sho
give dem a sharp appetite. See, it natural cause if you take
a tablespoon of dat bitter medicine three times a day like a
person tell you, it bound to swell your appetite. Yes,mam,
I know dat a mighty good mixture."

"Oh, my Lord, child, de people was sho wiser in olden
times den what dey be now. Dey been have all kind of signs
to forecast de times wid en dey been mighty true to de word,
too. Say, when you hear a cow low en cry so mournful like,
it ain' gwine be long fore you hear tell of a death."

"Den dere one bout de rain. Say, sometimes de old rain
crow stays in de air en hollers en if you don' look right
sharp, it gwine rain soon. Call him de rain crow. He hollers
mostly like dis, 'Goo-oop, goo-oop.' Like dat."

"De people used to have a bird for cold weather, too. Folks
say, 'Don' you hear dat cold bird? Look out, it gwine be cold
tomorrow.' De cold bird, he a brown bird. If you can see him,

Code No.
Project, 1885-(1)
Prepared by Annie Ruth Davis
Place, Marion, S.C.
Date, January 4, 1938

No. Words_____
Reduced from____words
Rewritten by

Page 6.   25

he a fine lookin bird, too. Yes'um, right large en strong
lookin, but don' nobody hardly ever see him dese days."

"En I reckon you hear talk bout dis one. Say, not to
wash on de first day of de New Year cause if you do, you
will wash some of your family out de pot. Say, somebody will
sho die. Dat right, too. Den if possible, must boil some old
peas on de first day of de New Year en must cook some hog jowl
in de pot wid dem. Must eat some of it, but don' be obliged
to eat it all. En ought to have everything clean up nicely
so as to keep clean all de year. Say, must always put de wash
out on de line to be sure de day fore New Years en have all
your garments clean."

"What my ideas bout de young folks dese days? Well, dey
young folks en dey ain' young folks, I say. Cose I don' bother
up wid dem none, but I think wid my own weak judgment, dey quite
different from when I come along. Folks is awful funny dis day
en time to my notion. Don' care what people see dem do no time.
I sho think dey worser den what dey used to be. De way I say dey
worser, I used to have to be back at such en such a time, if I
went off, but now dey go anytime dey want to en dey comes back
anytime dey want to. I sho think dey worser. De fact of it,
I know dey worser."

Source: Josephine Bacchus, colored, age 75-80, Marion, S.C.
          Personal interview by Annie Ruth Davis, Dec., 1937.

Project 1885-1
FOLKLORE
Spartanburg Dist.4
June 14, 1937

390163

Edited by:
Elmer Turnage

26

STORIES FROM EX-SLAVES

"I was born near Winnsboro, S.C., Fairfield County. I was
twelve years old the year the Confederate war started. My father
was John Ballard and my mother was Sallie Ballard. I had several
brothers and sisters. We belonged to Jim Aiken, a large land-
owner at Winnsboro. He owned land on which the town was built.
He had seven plantations. He was good to us and give us plenty to
eat, and good quarters to live in. His mistress was good, too;
but one of his sons, Dr. Aiken, whipped some of de niggers, lots.
One time he whipped a slave for stealing. Some of his land was
around four churches in Winnsboro.

"We was allowed three pounds o' meat, one quart o' molasses, grits and other things each week --- plenty for us to eat.

"When freedom come, he told us we was free, and if we
wanted to stay on with him, he would do the best he could for us.
Most of us stayed, and after a few months, he paid wages. After
eight months, some went to other places to work.

"The master's wife died and he married a daughter of Robert
Gillam and moved to Greenville, S.C.

"The master always had a very big garden with plenty of
vegetables. He had fifty hogs, and I helped mind the hogs. He
didn't raise much cotton, but raised lots of wheat and corn. He
made his own meal and flour from the mill on the creek; made
home-made clothes with cards and spinning wheels.

"They cooked in wide chimneys in a kitchen which was away
off from the big house. They used pots and skillets to cook with.

The hands got their rations every Monday night. They got their
clothes to wear which they made on old spinning wheels, and wove
them themselves.

"The master had his own tan yard and tanned his leather and
made shoes for his hands.

"He had several overseers, white men, and some negro foremen. They sometimes whipped the slaves, that is the overseers.
Once a nigger whipped the overseer and had to run away in the
woods and live so he wouldn't get caught. The nigger foremen looked after a set of slaves on any special work. They never worked at
night unless it was to bring in fodder or hay when it looked like
rain was coming. On rainy days, we shucked corn and cleaned up
around the place.

"We had old brick ovens, lots of 'em. Some was used to make
molasses from our own sugar cane we raised.

"The master had a 'sick-house' where he took sick slaves
for treatment, and kept a drug store there. They didn't use old-
time cures much, like herbs and barks, except sassafras root tea
for the blood.

"We didn't learn to read and write, but some learned after
the war.

"My father run the blacksmith shop for the master on the
place. I worked around the place. The patrollers were there and
we had to have a pass to get out any. The nigger children sometimes played out in the road and were chased by patrollers. The
children would run into the master's place and the patrollers
couldn't get them 'cause the master wouldn't let them. We had no
churches for slaves, but went to the white church and set in the
gallery. After freedom, niggers built 'brush harbors' on the place.

"Slaves carried news from one plantation to another by riding mules or horses. They had to be in quarters at night. I remember my mother rode side-saddle one Saturday night. I reckon she had a pass to go; she come back without being bothered.

"Some games children played was, hiding switches, marbles, and maybe others. Later on, some of de nigger boys started playing cards and got to gambling; some went to de woods to gamble.

"The old cotton gins on de farms were made of wooden screws, and it took all day to gin four bales o' cotton.

"I was one of the first trustees that helped build the first colored folks' church in the town of Greenwood. I am the only one now living. I married Alice Robinson, and had five sons and one daughter, and have five or six grandchildren.

"Abraham Lincoln, I think, was a good man; had a big reputation. Couldn't tell much about Jefferson Davis. Booker T. Washington --Everybody thinks he is a great man for the colored race.

"Of course I think slavery was bad. We is free now and better off to work. I think anybody who is any count can work and live by himself.

"I joined de church when I was 17 years old, because a big preaching was going on after freedom for the colored people.

"I think everybody should join the church and do right; can't get anywhere without it, and do good."

Source: William Ballard (88), Greenwood, S.C.
         Interviewed by: G.L. Summer, Newberry, S.C. (6/10/37)

CHARLEY BARBER

EX-SLAVE 81 YEARS OLD.

Charley Barber lives in a shanty kind of house, situated on a plot of ground containing two acres all his own. It is a mile and a half southeast of Winnsboro, S. C. He lives with an anaemic daughter, Maggie, whose chief interests are a number of cats, about the premises, and a brindled, crumple-horned cow that she ties out to graze every morning and milks at evening.

Charley is squat of figure, short neck, popeyed, and has white hair. He tills the two acres and produces garden truck that he finds a sale for among the employees of the Winnsboro mills, just across the railroad from his home. He likes to talk, and pricks up his ears,(so to speak),whenever anything is related as having occurred in the past. He will importune those present to hear his version of the event unusual.

"Well sah, dis is a pleasure to have you call 'pon me, howsomever it be unexpected dis mornin'. Shoo! (driving the chickens out of the house) Shoo! Git out of here and go scratch a livin' for them chickens dat's followin' you yet, and you won't wean and git to layin' again. Fust thing you know you'll be spoilin' de floor, when us is got company dis very minute. Scat! Maggie, git them cats out de chairs long 'nough for Mr. Wood to set in one whilst he's come to see me dis mornin'.

"And dat's it? You wants me to talk over de days dat am gone? How dis come 'bout and how dat come 'bout, from de day I was born, to dis very hour? Let's light up our smokestacks befo' us begin. Maybe you wants a drink of water. Maggie, fetch de water here!

"How old you think I is, sixty-five? My goodness! Do you hear dat Maggie? (Rubbing his hands; his eyes shining with pleasure) Take another look and make another guess. Seventy-five? You is growin' warm but you'll have to come again!

"Bless your soul Marse Wood, you know what old Mudder Shifton say? She 'low dat: 'In de year 1881, de world to an end will surely come'. I was twenty-five years old, when all de niggers and most of de white folks was believin' dat old lady and lookin' for de world to come to an end in 1881. Dat was de year dat I jined de church, 'cause I wanted to make sure dat if de end did come, I'd be caught up in dat rapture dat de white Methodist preacher was preachin' 'bout and explainin' to my marster and mistress at deir house on de piazza dat year.

"I is eighty-one years old. I was born up on de Wateree River, close to Great Falls. My marster was Ozmond Barber. My mistress was name Miss Elizabeth; her de wife of Marse Ozmond. My pappy was name Jacob. My mammy went by de name of Jemima. They both come from Africa where they was born. They was 'ticed on a ship, fetch 'cross de ocean to Virginny, fetch to Winnsboro by a slave drover, and sold to my marster's father. Dat what they tell me. When they was sailin' over, dere was five or six hundred others all together down under de first deck of de ship, where they was locked in. They never did talk lak de other slaves, could just say a few words, use deir hands, and make signs. They want deir collards, turnips, and deir 'tators, raw. They lak sweet milk so much they steal it.

"Pappy care nothin' 'bout clothes and wouldn't wear shoes in de winter time or any time. It was 'ginst de law to bring them over here when they did, I learn since. But what is de law now and what was de law then, when bright shiny money was in sight? Money make de automobile go. Money make de train go. Money make de mare go, and at dat time I 'spect money make de ships go.

Yes sir, they, my pappy and mammy, was just smuggled in dis part of de world, I bet you!

"War come on, my marster went out as a captain of de Horse Marines. A tune was much sung by de white folks on de place and took wid de niggers. It went lak dis:

'I'm Captain Jenks of de Horse Marines

I feed my horse on corn and beans.

Oh! I'm Captain Jenks of de Horse Marines

And captain in de army!'

"When de Yankees come they seem to have special vengeance for my white folks. They took everything they could carry off and burnt everything they couldn't carry off.

"Mistress and de chillun have to go to Chester to git a place to sleep and eat, wid kinfolks. De niggers just lay 'round de place 'til master rode in, after de war, on a horse; him have money and friends and git things goin' agin. I stay on dere 'til '76. Then I come to Winnsboro and git a job as section hand laborer on de railroad. Out of de fust money,--(I git paid off de pay train then; company run a special pay train out of Columbia to Charlotte. They stop at every station and pay de hands off at de rear end of de train in cash). Well, as I was a sayin': Out de fust money, I buys me a red shirt and dat November I votes and de fust vote I put in de box was for Governor Wade Hampton. Dat was de fust big thing I done.

"De nex' big thing I done was fall in love wid Mary Wylie. Dat come 'bout on de second pay day. De other nigger gals say her marry me for my money but I never have believed it. White ladies do dat 'kalkilating' trick sometime but you take a blue-gum nigger gal, all wool on de top of her head and lak to dance and jig wid her foots, to pattin' and fiddle music, her ain't

gonna have money in de back of her head when her pick out a man to marry.
Her gonna want a man wid muscles on his arms and back and I had them. Usin'
dat pick and shovel on de railroad just give me what it took to git Mary.
Us had ten chillun. Some dead, some marry and leave. My wife die year befo'
last. Maggie is puny, as you see, and us gits 'long wid de goodness of de
Lord and de white folks.

"I b'longs to de St. John Methodist Church in Middlesix, part of Winnsboro. They was havin' a rival (revival) meetin' de night of de earthquake,
last day of August, in 1886. Folks had hardly got over de scare of 1881, 'bout
de world comin' to an end. It was on Tuesday night, if I don't disremember,
'bout 9 o'clock. De preacher was prayin', just after de fust sermon, but him
never got to de amen part of dat prayer. Dere come a noise or rumblin', lak
far off thunder, seem lak it come from de northwest, then de church begin to
rock lak a baby's cradle. Dere was great excitement. Old Aunt Melvina holler:
'De world comin' to de end'. De preacher say: 'Oh, Lordy', and run out of de
pulpit. Everbody run out de church in de moonlight. When de second quake come,
'bout a minute after de fust, somebody started up de cry: 'De devil under de
church! De devil under de church! De devil gwine to take de church on his back
and run away wid de church!' People never stop runnin' 'til they got to de
court house in town. Dere they, 'clare de devil done take St. John's Church on
his back and fly away to hell wid it. Marse Henry Galliard make a speech and
tell them what it was and beg them to go home. Dat Mr. Skinner, de telegraph
man at de depot, say de main part of it was way down 'bout Charleston, too far
away for anybody to git hurt here, 'less a brick from a chimney fall on somebody's head. De niggers mostly believes what a fine man, lak Marse Henry, tell
them. De crowd git quiet. Some of them go home but many of them, down in de

low part of town, set on de railroad track in de moonlight, all night.
I was mighty sleepy de nex' mornin' but I work on de railroad track
just de same. Dat night folks come back to St. John's Church, find it
still dere, and such a outpourin' of de spirit was had as never was had
befo' or since.

"Just think! Dat has been fifty-one years ago. Them was de glorious
horse and buggy days. Dere was no air-ships, no autos and no radios. White
folks had horses to drive. Niggers had mules to ride to a baseball game, to
see white folks run lak de patarollers (patrollers) was after them and they
holler lak de world was on fire."

Project #1655
W. W. Dixon
Winnsboro, S. C.

390341

ED BARBER

EX-SLAVE 77 YEARS OLD.

Ed Barber lives in a small one-room house in the midst of a cotton field
on the plantation of Mr. A. M. Owens, ten miles southeast of Winnsboro, S. C.
He lives alone and does his own cooking and housekeeping. He is a bright mulatto,
has an erect carriage and posture, appears younger than his age, is intelligent
and enjoys recounting the tales of his lifetime. His own race doesn't give him
much countenance. His friends in the old days of reconstruction were white people. He presumes on such past affiliation and considers himself better than the
full-blooded Negro.

"It's been a long time since I see you. Maybe you has forgot but I ain't
forgot de fust time I put dese lookers on you, in '76. Does you 'members dat **day**?
It was in a piece of pines beyond de Presbyterian Church, in Winnsboro, S. C. Us
both had red shirts. You was a ridin' a gray pony and I was a ridin' a red mule,
sorrel like. You say dat wasn't '76? Well, how come it wasn't? Ouillah Harrison,
another nigger, was dere, though he was a man. Both of us got to arguin'. He
'low he could vote for Hampton and I couldn't, 'cause I wasn't 21. You say it **was**
'78 'stead of '76, dat day in de pines when you was dere? Well! Well! I sho'
been thinkin' all dis time it was '76.

" 'Member de fight dat day when Mr. Pole Barnadore knock Mr. Blanchard
down, while de speakin' was a gwine on? You does? Well, us come to common 'gree-
ment on dat, bless God!

"Them was scary times! Me bein' just half nigger and half white man, I knowed which side de butter was on de bread. Who I see dere? Well, dere was a string
of red shirts a mile long, dat come into Winnsboro from White Oak. And another

from Flint Hill, over de Pea Ferry road, a mile long. De barrooms of de town
did a big business dat day. Seem lak it was de fashion to git drunk all 'long
them days.

"Them red shirts was de monkey wrench in de cotton-gin of de carpet bag
party. I's here to tell you. If a nigger git hungry, all he have to do is go
to de white folk's house, beg for a red shirt, and explain hisself a democrat.
He might not git de shirt right then but he git his belly full of everything de
white folks got, and de privilege of comin' to dat trough sometime agin.

"You wants me to tell you 'bout who I is, where I born, and how old I is?
Well, just cross examine me and I'll tell you de facts as best I knows how.

"I was born twelve miles east of Winnsboro, S. C. My marster say it was
de 18th of January, 1860.

"My mother name Ann. Her b'long to my marster, James Barber. Dat's not
a fair question when you ask me who my daddy was. Well, just say he was a white
man and dat my mother never did marry nobody, while he lived. I was de onliest
child my mother ever had.

"After freedom my mother raised me on de Marse Adam Barber place, up by
Rocky Mount and Mitford. I stayed dere 'til all de 'citement of politics die
down. My help was not wanted so much at de 'lection boxes, so I got to roamin'
'round to fust one place and then another. But wheresomever I go, I kept a thinkin' 'bout Rosa and de ripe may-pops in de field in cotton pickin' time. I landed
back to de Barber place and after a skirmish or two wid de old folks, marry de
gal de Lord always 'tended for me to marry. Her name was Rosa Ford. You ask me
if she was pretty? Dat's a strange thing. Do you ever hear a white person say
a colored woman is pretty? I never have but befo' God when I was trampin' 'round
Charleston, dere was a church dere called St. Mark, dat all de society folks of

my color went to. No black nigger welcome dere, they told me. Thinkin' as
how I was bright 'nough to git in, I up and goes dere one Sunday. Ah, how
they did carry on, bow and scrape and ape de white folks. I see some pretty
feathers, pretty fans, and pretty women dere! I was uncomfortable all de
time though, 'cause they was too 'hifalootin' in de ways, in de singin', and
all sorts of carryin' ons.

"Glad you fetch me back to Rosa. Us marry and had ten chillun. Francis,
Thompkins, William, Jim, Levi, Ab and Oz is dead. Katie marry a Boykin and is
livin' in New York. My wife, Rosa, die on dis place of Mr. Owens.

"I lives in a house by myself. I hoes a little cotton, picks plums and
blackberries but dewberries 'bout played out.

"My marster, James Barber, went through de Civil War and died. I begs
you, in de name of de good white folks of '76 and Wade Hampton, not to forget
me in dis old age pension business.

"What I think of Abe Lincoln? I think he was a poor buckra white man, to
de likes of me. Although, I 'spects Mr. Lincoln meant well but I can't help
but wish him had continued splittin' them fence rails, which they say he knowed
all 'bout, and never took a hand in runnin' de government of which he knowed
nothin' 'bout. Marse Jeff Davis was all right, but him oughta got out and fought
some, lak General Lee, General Jackson and 'Poleon Bonaparte. Us might have won
de
de war if he had turned up at some of/big battles lak Gettysburg, 'Chickenmaroger',
and 'Applemattox'. What you think 'bout dat?

"Yes sah, I has knowed a whole lot of good white men. Marse General Bratton,
Marse Ed R. Mobley, Marse Will Durham, dat owned dis house us now settin' in, and
Dr. Henry Gibson. Does I know any good colored men? I sho' does! Dere's Profes-

sor Benjamin Russell at Blackstock. You knows him. Then dere was Ouillah Harrison, dat own a four-hoss team and a saddle hoss, in red shirt days. One time de brass band at Winnsboro, S. C. wanted to go to Camden, S. C. to play at de speakin' of Hampton. He took de whole band from Winnsboro to Camden, dat day, free of charge. Ah! De way dat band did play all de way to Ridgeway, down de road to Longtown, cross de Camden Ferry, and right into de town. Dere was horns a blowin', drums a beatin', and people a shoutin': 'Hurrah for Hampton!' Some was a singin': 'Hang Dan Chamberlain on a Sour Apple Tree'. Ouillah come home and found his wife had done had a boy baby. What you reckon? He name dat boy baby, Wade Hampton. When he come home to die, he lay his hand on dat boy's head and say: 'Wade, 'member who you name for and always vote a straight out democrat ticket'. Which dat boy did!"

MILLIE BARBER

EX-SLAVE 82 YEARS OLD.

"Hope you find yourself well dis mornin', white folks. I's
just common; 'spect I eats too much yesterday. You know us celebrated
yesterday, 'cause it was de Fourth of July. Us had a good dinner on
dis 2,000 acre farm of Mr. Owens. God bless dat white boss man! What
would us old no 'count niggers do widout him? Dere's six or seven,
maybe eight of us out here over eighty years old. 'Most of them is like
me, not able to hit a lick of work, yet he take care of us; he sho' does.

"Mr. Owens not a member of de church but he allowed dat he done
found out dat it more blessed to give than to receive, in case like us.

"You wants to know all 'bout de slavery time, de war, de Ku Kluxes
and everything? My tongue too short to tell you all dat I knows. However,
if it was as long as my stockin's, I could tell you a trunk full of good
and easy, bad and hard, dat dis old life-stream have run over in eighty-
two years. I's hoping to reach at last them green fields of Eden of de
Promise Land. 'Scuse me ramblin' 'round, now just ask me questions; I
bet I can answer all you ask.

"My pa name, Tom McCullough; him was a slave of old Marster John
McCullough, whose big two-story house is de oldest in Fairfield County.
It stands today on a high hill, just above de banks of Dutchman Creek.
Big road run right by dat house. My mammy name, Nicie. Her b'long to
de Weir family; de head of de family die durin' de war of freedom. I's
not supposed to know all he done, so I'll pass over dat. My mistress
name, Eliza; good mistress. Have you got down dere dat old marster just

took sick and die, 'cause he wasn't touched wid a bullet nor de life slashed out of him wid a sword?

"Well, my pa b'longin' to one man and my mammy b'longin' to another, four or five miles apart, caused some confusion, mix-up, and heartaches. My pa have to git a pass to come to see my mammy. He come sometimes widout de pass. Patrollers catch him way up de chimney hidin' one night; they stripped him right befo' mammy and give him thirty-nine lashes, wid her cryin' and a hollerin' louder than he did.

"Us lived in a log house; handmade bedstead, wheat straw mattress, cotton pillows, plenty coverin' and plenty to eat, sich as it was. Us never git butter or sweet milk or coffee. Dat was for de white folks but in de summer time, I minds de flies off de table wid the peafowl feather brush and eat in de kitchen just what de white folks eat; them was very good eatin's I's here for to tell you. All de old slaves and them dat worked in de field, got rations and de chillun were fed at de kitchen out-house. What did they git? I 'members they got peas, hog meat, corn bread, 'lasses, and buttermilk on Sunday, then they got greens, turnips, taters, shallots, collards, and beans through de week. They were kept fat on them kind of rations.

"De fact is I can't 'member us ever had a doctor on de place; just a granny was enough at child birth. Slave women have a baby one day, up and gwine 'round de next day, singin' at her work lak nothin' unusual had happened.

"Did I ever git a whippin'? Dat I did. How many times? More than I can count on fingers and toes. What I git a whippin' for? Oh, just one thing, then another. One time I break a plate while washin' dishes

and another time I spilt de milk on de dinin' room floor. It was always
for somethin', sir. I needed de whippin'.

"Yes sir, I had two brothers older than me; one sister older
than me and one brother younger than me.

"My young marster was killed in de war. Their names was Robert,
Smith, and Jimmie. My young mistress, Sarah, married a Sutton and moved
to Texas. Nancy marry Mr. Wade Rawls. Miss Janie marry Mr. Hugh Melving.
At this marriage my mammy was give to Miss Janie and she was took to Texas
wid her young baby, Isaiah, in her arms. I have never seen or heard tell
of them from dat day to dis.

"De Yankees come and burn de gin-house and barns. Open de smoke-
house, take de meat, give de slaves some, shoot de chickens, and as de
mistress and girls beg so hard, they left widout burnin' de dwellin' house.

"My oldest child, Alice, is livin' and is fifty-one years old de
10th of dis last May gone. My first husband was Levi Young; us lived wid
Mr. Knox Picket some years after freedom. We moved to Mr. Rubin Lumpkin's
plantation, then to George Boulwares. Well, my husband die and I took a
fool notion, lak most widows, and got into slavery again. I marry Prince
Barber; Mr. John Hollis, Trial Justice, tied de knot. I loved dat young
nigger more than you can put down dere on paper, I did. He was black and
shiny as a crow's wing. Him was white as snow to dese old eyes. Ah, the
joy, de fusses, de ructions, de beatin's, and de makin'ups us had on de
Ed Shannon place where us lived. Us stay dere seven long years.

"Then de Klu Kluxes comed and lak to scared de life out of me.
They ask where Prince was, searched de house and go away. Prince come
home 'bout daylight. Us took fright, went to Marster Will Durham's and

asked for advice and protection. Marster Will Durham fixed it up. Next
year us moved to dis place, he own it then but Marster Arthur Owens owns
it now. Dere is 2,000 acres in dis place and another 1,000 acres in de
Rubin Lumpkin place 'joinin' it.

"Prince die on dis place and I is left on de mercy of Marster
Arthur, livin' in a house wid two grandchillun, James twelve years, and
John Roosevelt Barber, eight years old. Dese boys can work a little.
They can pick cotton and tote water in de field for de hands and marster
say: 'Every little help'.

"My livin' chillun ain't no help to me. Dere's Willie, I don't
know where he is. Prince is wid Mr. Freeman on de river. Maggie is here
on de place but she no good to me.

"I 'spect when I gits to drawin' down dat pension de white folks
say is comin', then dere will be more folks playin' in my backyard than dere
is today."

ANDERSON BATES

EX-SLAVE 87 YEARS OLD.

Anderson Bates lives with his son-in-law and daughter, Ed and Dora
Owens, in a three-room frame house, on lands of Mr. Dan Heyward, near the
Winnsboro Granite Company, Winnsboro, S. C. Anderson and his wife occupy
one of the rooms and his rent is free. His son-in-law has regular employment
at the Winnsboro Cotton Mills. His wife, Carrie, looks after the house. Anderson and his daughter, Dora, are day laborers on the neightborhood farms, but
he is able to do very little work.

"I was born on de old Dr. Furman place, near Jenkinsville, S. C.,
in de year, 1850. My pappy was name Nat and mammy name Winnie. They was slaves
of old Dr. Furman, dat have a big plantation, one hundred slaves, and a whole
lot of little slave chillun, dat him wouldn't let work. They run 'round in de
plum thickets, blackberry bushes, hunt wild strawberries, blow cane whistles,
and have a good time.

"De old Dr. Furman house is ramshackle but it is still standin' out
dere and is used as a shelter for sawmill hands dat is cuttin' down de big pines
and sawin' them on de place.

"Where did my pappy and mammy come from? Mammy was born a slave in
de Furman family in Charleston, but pappy was bought out of a drove dat a Balti-
more speculator fetch from Maryland long befo' de war. Doctor practice all
'round and 'bout Monticello, happen 'long one day, see my pappy and give a thousand dollars for him, to dat speculator. I thank God for dat!

"Dr. Furman, my old marster, have a brudder called Jim, dat run de
Furman School, fust near Winnsboro, then it move to Greenville, S. C.

"My mistress name Nancy. Her was of de quality. Her voice was soft and quiet to de slaves. Her teach us to sing:

"Dere is a happy land, far, far 'way,

Where bright angels stand, far, far 'way,

Oh! How them angels sing!

Oh! How them bells ring!

In dat happy land, far, far 'way!'

"Dere was over a thousand acres, maybe two thousand in dat old Furman place. Them sawmill folks give $30,000.00 for it, last year.

"My pappy and mammy was field hands. My brudders and sisters was: Liddie, Millie, Ria, Ella, Harriet, Thomas, Smith, and Marshall. All dead but me and Marshall.

"I was fifteen when de Yankees come thru. They took off everything, hosses, mules, cows, sheep, goats, turkeys, geese, and chickens. Hogs? Yes sah, they kill hogs and take off what parts they want and leave other parts bleedin' on de yard. When they left, old marster have to go up into Union County for rations.

"Dat funny, you wants to set down dere 'bout my courtship and weddin'? Well, sir, I stay on de old plantation, work for my old marster, de doctor, and fell head over heels in love wid Carrie. Dere was seven more niggers a flyin' 'round dat sugar lump of a gal in de night time when I breezes in and takes charge of de fireside sheer. I knocks one down one night, kick another out de nex' night, and choke de stuffin' out of one de nex' night. I landed de three-leg stool on de head of de fourth one, de last time. Then de others carry deir 'fections to some other place than Carrie's house. Us have some hard words 'bout my bad manners, but I told her dat I couldn't 'trol my feelin's wid them fools a settin' 'round dere gigglin' wid her. I go clean crazy!

"Then us git married and go to de ten-acre quarry wid Mr. Anderson. I work dere a while and then go to Captain Macfie, then to his son, Wade, and then to Marse Rice Macfie. Then I go back to de quarry, drill and git out stone. They pay me $3.50 a day 'til de Parr Shoals Power come in wid 'lectric power drills and I was cut down to eighty cents a day. Then I say: 'Old grey hoss! Damn 'lectric toolin', I's gwine to leave.' I went to Hopewell, Virginia, and work wid de DuPonts for five years. War come on and they ask me to work on de acid area. De atmosphere dere tear all de skin off my face and arms, but I stuck it out to de end of de big war, for $7.20 a day. I drunk a good deal of liquor then, but I sent money to Carrie all de time and fetch her a roll every fourth of July and on Christmas. After de war they dismantle de plant and I come back to work for Mr. Eleazer, on de Saluda River for $2.00 a day, for five years.

"Carrie have chillun by me. Dere was Anderson, my son, ain't see him in forty years. Essie, my daughter, marry Herbert Perrin. Dora, another daughter, marry Ed Owens. Ed makes good money workin' at de factory in Winnsboro. They have seven chillun. Us tries to keep them chillun in school but they don't have de good times I had when a child, a eatin' cracklin' bread and buttermilk, liver, pig-tails, hog-ears and turnip greens.

"Does I 'member anything 'bout de Klu Kluxes? Jesus, yes! My old marster, de doctor, in goin' 'round, say out loud to people dat Klu Kluxes was doin' some things they ought not to do, by 'stortin' money out of niggers just 'cause they could.

"When he was gone to Union one day, a low-down pair of white men come, wid false faces, to de house and ask where Dick Bell was. Miss Nancy say her

don't know. They go hunt for him. Dick made a bee-line for de house. They
pull out hoss pistols, fust time,'pow'. Dick run on, secon' time, 'pow'.
Dick run on, third time, 'pow' and as Dick reach de front yard de ball from
de third shot keel him over lak a hit rabbit. Old miss run out but they git
him. Her say: 'I give you five dollars to let him 'lone.' They say: 'Not
'nough.' Her say: 'I give you ten dollars.' They say: 'Not 'nough.' Her
say: 'I give you fifteen dollars.' They say: 'Not 'nough.' Her say: 'I
give you twenty-five dollars.' They take de money and say: 'Us'll be back
tomorrow for de other Dick.' They mean Dick James.

"Nex' day, us see them a comin' again. Dick James done load up de
shotgun wid buckshot. When they was comin' up de front steps, Uncle Dick
say to us all in de big house: 'Git out de way!' De names of de men us
find out afterwards was Bishop and Fitzgerald. They come up de steps, wid
Bishop in de front. Uncle Dick open de door, slap dat gun to his shoulder,
and pull de trigger. Dat man Bishop hollers: 'Oh Lordy.' He drop dead and
lay dere 'til de coroner come. Fitzgerald leap 'way. They bring Dick to
jail, try him right in dat court house over yonder. What did they do wid him?
Well, when Marse Bill Stanton, Marse Elisha Ragsdale and Miss Nancy tell 'bout
it all from de beginnin' to de end, de judge tell de jury men dat Dick had a
right to protect his home, and hisself, and to kill dat white man and to turn
him loose. Dat was de end of de Klu Kluxes in Fairfield."

Project 1885 - 1
From Field Notes
Spartanburg, Dist.4
April 28. 1937

390035 Vol 5

[Amison]

Edited by:
Elmer Turnage

46

Later

FOLK LORE: FOLK TALES (negro)

"I sho members when de soldiers come home from de war.
All de women folks, both black as well as shite wuz so glad to see
'em back dat we jus jumped up and hollered 'Oh, Lawdy, God bless
you.' When you would look around a little, you would see some wid
out an arm or maybe dey would be a walkin' wid a cruch or a stick.
Den you would cry some wid out lettin your white folks see you. But
Jane, de worsest time of all fer us darkies wuz when de Ku Klux
killed Dan Black. We wuz little chilluns a playin' in Dans house.
We didn't know he had done nothin' ginst de white folks. Us wuz a
playin by de fire jus as nice when something hit on de wall. Dan,
he jump up and try to git outten de winder. A white spooky thing
had done come in de doo' right by me. I was so scairt dat I could
not git up. I had done fell straight out on de flo'. When Dan stick
his head outten dat winder something say bang and he fell right down
in de flo'. I crawles under de bed. When I got dar, all de other
chilluns wuz dar to, lookin' as white as ashed dough from hickory
wood. Us peeped out and den us duck under de bed agin. Ain't no
bed ebber done as much good as dat one. Den a whole lot of dem
come in de house. De wuz all white and scairy lookin'. It still
makes de shivvers run down my spine and here I is ole and you all
a settin' around wid me and two mo' wars done gone since dat awful
time. Dan Black, he wo'nt no mo' kaise de took dat nigger and
hung him to a simmon tree. Dey would not let his folks take him
down either. He jus stayed dar till he fell to pieces.

"After dat when us chilluns seed de Ku Klux a comin',
us would take an' run breadneck speed to de nearest wood. Dar we
would stay till dey wuz plum out o' sight and you could not even
hear de horses feet. Dem days wuz wors'n de war. Yes Lawd, dey wuz
worse'n any war I is ebber heard of.

"Was not long after dat fore de spooks wuz a gwine round
ebber whar. When you would go out atter dark, somethin' would start
to a haintin' ye. You would git so scairt dat you would mighty ni
run every time you went out atter dark; even iffin you didn't see
nothin'. Chile, don't axe me what I seed. Atter all dat killin' and
a burnin' you know you wuz bliged to see things wid all dem spirits
in distress a gwine all over de land. You see, it is like dis, when
a man gits killed befo he is done what de good Lawd intended fer
him to do, he comes back here and tries to find who done him wrong.
I mean he don' come back hisself, but de spirit, it is what comes
and wanders around. Course, it can't do nothin', so it jus scares
folks and haints dem."

SOURCE: "Aunt" Millie Bates, 25 Hamlet street, Union, S.C.
        Interviewer: Caldwell Sims, Union, S.C.

Project #1655
Mrs. Genevieve W. Chandler
Murrells Inlet, S. C.
Georgetown County

VISIT WITH UNCLE WELCOME BEES - - - AGE 104 YEARS

The road is perfectly camouflaged from the King's Highway by wild plums
that lap overhead. Only those who have traveled this way before could locate
the 'turn in' to Uncle Welcome's house. When you have turned in and come suddenly out from the plum thicket you find your road winding along with cultivated
patches on the left -- corn and peas -- a fenced-in garden, the palings riven
out by hand, and thick dark woods on the left. A lonesome, untenanted cabin is
seemingly in the way but your car swings to the left instead of climbing the
door-step and suddenly you find you are facing a bog. The car may get through;
it may not. So you switch off and just sit a minute, seeing how the land lies.
A great singing and chopping of wood off to the left have kept the inmates from
hearing the approach of a car. When you rap therefore you hear, 'Come in'.

A narrow hall runs through to the back porch and off this hall on your
right opens a door from beyond which comes a very musical squeaking -- you
know a rocking chair is going hard -- even before you see it in motion with
a fuzzy little head that rests on someone's shoulder sticking over the top.
And the fuzzy head which in size is like a small five-cent cocoanut, belongs to
Uncle Welcome's great-grand. On seeing a visitor the grand, the mother of the
infant, rises and smiles greeting, and, learning your errand, points back to the
kitchen to show where Uncle Welcome sits. You step down one step and ask him
if you may come in and he pats a chair by his side. The old man isn't so spry

VISIT WITH UNCLE WELCOME BEES ---AGE 104 YEARS

as he was when you saw him in the fall; the winter has been hard. But here

it is warm again and at most four in the April afternoon, he sits over his

plate of hopping John -- he and innumerable flies.   At his feet, fairly un-

der the front of a small iron stove, sits another great-grand with a plate of

peas between her legs. Peas and rice, 'hopping John'. (Someone says peas

and hominy cooked together makes "limping Lizzie in the Low-Country. But

that is another story.)

                    * * * * * * * * * * * * * *

    "Uncle Welcome, isn't Uncle Jeemes Stuart the oldest liver on Sandy Island?"

Welcome: "Jeemes Stuart? I was married man when he born. Jeemes rice-field .

(Worker in rice-field) posed himself. In all kinds of weather. Cut you down,

down, down. Jeemes second wife gal been married before but he husband dead.

    "I couldn't tell the date or time I born. Your Maussa (Master) take it

down. When I been marry, Dr. Ward Fadder (Father) aint been marry yet. My

mother had twelve head born oatland. He bought my mother from Virginia. Dolly.

Sam he husband name. Sam come from same course. When my mother been bought, he

been young woman. Work in rice. Plow right now (Meaning April is time to plow

rice fields). I do carpenter work and mind horse for plantation. Come from

Georgetown in boat. Have you own carriage. Go anywhere you want to go. Oatland

church build for colored people and po-buckra. I helped build that church. The

Project #1655 .
Mrs. Genevieve W. Chandler
Murrells Inlet, S. C.
Georgetown County

FOLKLORE

Page   3   *   50

VISIT WITH UNCLE WELCOME BEES --- AGE 104 YEARS

boss man, Mr. Bettman. My son Isaac sixty-nine. If him sixty-nine, I one

hundred four. That's my record. Maussa didn't low you to marry till you

twenty-two. Ben Allston own Turkey Hill. When him dead, I was twelve years

old. Me! (Knocking his chest)"

> Welcome Bees --
>
> Parkersville, S. C.
>
> (Near Waverly Mills, S. C.)
>
> Age 104.

Project #1655
W. W. Dixon
Winnsboro, S. C.

390258   :   51

ANNE BELL

EX-SLAVE 83 YEARS OLD.
(near Winnsboro, S.C.)

Anne Bell lives with her niece, in a one-room annex to a two-room frame house, on the plantation of Mr. Lake Howze, six miles west of Winnsboro, S. C. Her niece's husband, Golden Byrd, is a share-cropper on Mr. Howze's place. The old lady is still spry and energetic about the cares of housekeeping and attention to the small children of her niece. She is a delightful old lady and well worth her keep in the small chores she undertakes and performs in the household.

"My marster was John Glazier Rabb; us call him Marse Glazier. My mistress was Nancy Kincaid Watts; us call her Miss Nancy. They lived on a big plantation in Fairfield County and dere I come into dis world, eighty-three years ago, 10th day of April past.

"My pappy name just Andy but after de freedom, he took de name of Andrew Watts. My old mammy was Harriett but she come to you if you calls her Hattie. My brudders was Jake and Rafe. My sister name Charity. They all dead and gone to glory long time ago; left me here 'lone by myself and I's settin' here tellin' you 'bout them.

"My mammy was de cook at de 'Big House' for marster, Miss Nancy, and de chillun. Let me see if I can call them over in my mind. Dere was Marse John, went off to de war, color bearer at Seven Pines. Yes sir, him was killed wid de colors a flyin' in his hand. Heard tell of it many times. He lies right now in de old Buck Church graveyard. De pine trees, seven of them, cry and sob 'round him every August 6th; dat's de day he was killed. Oh, my God!

"Marse James went wid old Colonel Rion. They say he got shot but bullets couldn't kill him. No, bless God! Him comed back. Then come Marse Clarence. He went wid Captain Jim Macfie, went through it all and didn't get a scratch. Next was Miss Jesse. Then come Marse Horace, and Miss Nina. Us chillun all played together. Marse Horace is livin' yet and is a fine A. R. P. preacher of de Word. Miss Nina a rich lady, got plantation but live 'mong de big bugs in Winnsboro. She married Mr. Castles; she is a widow now. He was a good man, but he dead now.

"De one I minds next, is Charlie. I nussed him. He married Colonel Province's daughter. Dat's all I can call to mind, right now.

"Course de white folks I b'longs to, had more slaves than I got fingers and toes; whole families of them. De carpenter and de blacksmith on de place made de bedsteads. Us had good wheat straw mattresses to sleep on; cotton quilts, spreads, and cotton pillows. No trouble to sleep but it was hard to hear dat white overseer say at day break: 'Let me hear them foots hit de floor and dat befo' I go! Be lively! Hear me?' And you had to answer, 'Yas sah', befo' he'd move on to de nex' house. I does 'member de parts of de bed, was held together by wooden pins. I sho' 'members dat!

"Mammy Harriett was de cook. I didn't done no work but 'tend to de chillun and tote water.

"Money? Go 'way from here, boss! Lord, no sir, I never saw no money. What I want wid it anyhow?

"How did they feed us? Had better things to eat then, than now and more different kind of somethin's. Us had pears, 'lasses, shorts, middlings of de wheat, corn bread, and all kinds of milk and vegetables.

"Got a whuppin' once. They wanted me to go after de turkeys and I didn't want to go past de graveyard, where de turkeys was. I sho' didn't want to go by them graves. I's scared now to go by a graveyard in de dark. I took de whuppin' and somebody else must have got de turkeys. Sho' I didn't drive them up!

"Slaves spun de thread, loomed de cloth, and made de clothes for de plantation. Don't believe I had any shoes. I was just a small gal anyhow then, didn't need them and didn't want them.

"Yes, I's seen nigger women plow. Church? I wouldn't fool you, all de slaves big enough and not sick, had to go to church on de Sabbath.

"They give us a half Saturday, to do as we like.

"I was 'bout ten years old when de Yankees come. They was full to de brim wid mischief. They took de frocks out de presses and put them on and laugh and carry on powerful. Befo' they went they took everything. They took de meat and 'visions out de smoke-house, and de 'lasses, sugar, flour, and meal out de house. Killed de pigs and cows, burnt de gin-house and cotton, and took off de live stock, geese, chickens and turkeys.

"After de freedom, I stayed on wid mammy right dere, 'til I married Levi Bell. I's had two chillun. Dis my granddaughter, I visitin'. I never 'spects to have as good a home as I had in slavery time, 'til I gits my title to dat mansion in de sky. Dats de reason I likes to sing dat old plantation spiritual, 'Swing Low Sweet Chariot, Jesus Gwinter Carry me Home'. Does I believe in 'ligion? What else good for colored folks? I ask you if dere ain't a heaven, what's colored folks got to look forward to? They can't git anywhere down here. De only joy they can have here,

is servin' and lovin'; us can git dat in 'ligion but dere is a limit
to de nigger in everything else. Course I knows my place in dis world;
I 'umbles myself here to be 'zalted up yonder."

Project 1885-1
FOLKLORE
Spartanburg, Dist.4
July 26, 1937

390242

Edited by:
Elmer Turnage

55

SLAVERY REMINISCENCES

"I was raised in the wood across the road about 200 yards from here. I was very mischievous. My parents were honest and were Christians. I loved them very much. My father was William Bevis, who died at the age of eighty. Miss Zelia Hames of Pea Ridge was my mother. My parents are buried at Bethlehem Methodist Church. I was brought up in Methodism and I do not know anything else. I had two brothers and four sisters. My twin sister died last April 1937. She was Fannie Holcombe. I was in bed with pneumonia at the time of her death and of course I could not go to the funeral. For a month, I was unconscious.

"When I was a little girl I played 'Andy-over' with a ball, in the moonlight. Later I went to parties and dances. Calico, chambric and gingham were the materials which our party dresses were made of.

"My grandmother, Mrs. Phoebe Bevis used to tell Revolutionary stories and sing songs that were sung during that period. Grandmother knew some Tories. She always told me that old Nat Gist was a Tory ... that is the way he got rich.

"Hampton was elected governor the morning my mother died. Father went in his carriage to Jonesville to vote for Hampton. We all thought that Hampton was fine.

"When I was a school girl I used the blue back speller. My sweetheart's name was Ben Harris. We went to Bethlehem to school. Jeff and Bill Harris were our teachers. I was thirteen.

We went together for six years. The Confederate War commenced.
He was very handsome. He had black eyes and black hair. I had
seven curls on one side of my head and seven on the other. He
was twenty-four when he joined the "Boys of Sixteen'.

"He wanted to marry me then, but father would not let us
marry. He kissed me good bye and went off to Virginia. He was
a picket and was killed while on duty at Mars Hill. Bill Harris
was in a tent near-by and heard the shot. He brought Ben home.
I went to the funeral. I have never been much in-love since then.

"I hardly ever feel sad. I did not feel especially sad
during the war. I made socks, gloves and sweaters for the Confederate soldiers and also knitted for the World War soldiers.
During the war, there were three looms and three shuttles in
our house.

"I went often to the muster grounds at Kelton to see the
soldiers drill and to flirt my curls at them. Pa always went
with me to the muster field. Once he invited four recruits to
dine with us. We had a delicious supper. That was before the
Confederacy was paralyzed. Two darkies waited on our table that
night, Dorcas and Charlotte. A fire burned in our big fireplace and a lamp hung over the table. After supper was over, we
all sat around the fire in its flickering light.

"My next lover was Jess Holt and he was drowned in the
Mississippi River. He was a carpenter and was building a warf
on the river. He fell in and was drowned in a whirlpool.

Source: Miss Caroline Bevis (W. 96), County Home, Union, S.C.
         Interviewer: Caldwell Sims, Union, S.C. (7/13/37)

Code No.
Project, 1885-(1)
Prepared by Annie Ruth Davis
Place, Marion, S.C.
Date, June 21, 1937

No. ~~Words~~
Reduced from ___ words
Rewritten by
Page 1.

57

MAGGIE BLACK
Ex-Slave, 79 years

390287

"Honey, I don' know wha' to tell yuh 'bout dem times
back dere. Yuh see I wuz jes uh young child when de free
war close en I ain' know much to tell yuh. I born o'er de
river dere to Massa Jim Wilkerson plantation. Don' know
wha' 'come uv my ole Massa chillun a'ter dey head been gone.
Yuh see, honey, Massa Jim Wilkerson hab uh heap uv slave en
he hire my mudder out to Colonel Durant place right down de
road dere whey Miss Durant lib now. Coase I been back o'er
de river to visit 'mongest de peoples dere a'ter freedom wuz
'clare, but I ain' ne'er lib dere no more."

"Gawd been good to me, honey. I been heah uh long ole
time en I can' see mucha dese days, but I gettin''long sorta
so - so. I wuz train up to be uh nu'se 'oman en I betcha I
got chillun more den any 60 year ole 'bout heah now dat I
nu'se when dey wuz fust come heah. No, honey, ain' got no
chillun uv me own. Aw my chillun white lak yuh."

"No, no'mam, dey wear long ole frock den en uh girl
comin' on dere when dey ge' to be any kind uv uh girl, dey
put dat frock down. Oh, my child, dey can' ge' em short
'nough dese days. Ain' hab nuthin but uh string on dese day
en time. Dey use'er wear dem big ole hoop skirt dat sit out
broad lak from de ankle en den dey wear little panty dat
show down twixt dey skirt en dey ankle. Jes tie em 'round
dey knees wid some sorta string en le' em show dat way 'bout

Code No.
Project, 1885-(1)
Prepared by Annie Ruth Davis
Place, Marion, S.C.
Date, June 21, 1937

No. Words_____
Reduced from____words
Rewritten by_____
Page 2.

> 58

dey ankle. I 'member we black chillun'ud go in de woods en
ge' wild grape vine en bend em round en put em under us
skirt en make it stand out big lak. Hadder hab uh big ole
ring fa de bottom uv de skirt en den one uh little bit
smaller eve'y time dey ge' closer to de waist. Ne'er hab
none tall in de waist cause dat wuz s'ppose to be little
bitty t'ing."

"Dey weave aw de cloth dey use den right dere on de
plantation. Wear cotton en woolens aw de time den. Coase
de Madam, she could go en ge' de finest kind uv silk cause
mos' uv her t'ing come from 'broad. Child, I c'n see my
ole mammy how she look workin' dat spinning wheel jes uz
good uz ef dat day wuz dis day right heah. She set dere at
dat ole spinning wheel en take one shettle en t'row it one
way en den anmuder de udder way en pull dat t'ing en make
it tighter en tighter. Sumptin say zum, zum, zum, en den
yuh hadder work yuh feet dere too. Dat wuz de way dey make
dey cloth dat day en time."

"Honey, peoples hadder work dey hand fa eve'yt'ing dey
hab mos' den. Dey grew dey own rice right dere on de
plantation in dem days. Hadder plant it on some uv de land
wha' wuz weter den de udder land wus. Dey hadder le' de rice
ge' good en ripe en den dey'ud cut it en hab one uv dem big
rice whipping days. Heap uv people come from plantation aw

Code No.
Project, 1885-(1)
Prepared by Annie Ruth Davis
Place, Marion, S.C.
Date, June 21, 1937

No. Words_____
Reduced from_____words
Rewritten by
Page 3.

59

'bout en help whip dat rice. Dey jes take de rice en beat it
'cross some hoss dat dey hab fix up somewhey dere on de
plantation. Honey, dey hab hoss jes lak dese hoss yuh see
carpenter use 'bout heah dese days. Dey'ud hab hundreds uv
bushels uv dat rice dere. Den when dey ge' t'rough, dey hab
big supper dere fa aw dem wha' whip rice. Gi'e em aw de rice
en hog head dey is e'er wan'. Man, dey'ud hab de nicest kind
uv music dere. Knock dem bones togedder en slap en pat dey
hands to aw kind uv pretty tune."

"Den dey hab rice mortars right dere on de plantation
wha' dey fix de rice in jes uz nice. Now dey hab to take it
to de mill. Yuh see dey hab uh big block outer in de yard
wid uh big hole in it dat dey put de rice in en take dese
t'ing call pestles en beat down on it en dat wha' knock de
shaft offen it. Coase dey ne'er hab no nice pretty rice lak
yuh see dese days cause it wusn't uz white uz de rice dat dey
hab 'bout heah dis day en time, but it wuz mighty sweet rice,
honey, mighty sweet rice."

"No'mam, didn't hab no schools tall den. Ne'er gi'e de
colored peoples no l'arnin' no whey 'fore freedom 'clare.
Wha' little l'arnin' come my way wuz wha' I ge' when I stay
wid Miss Martha Leggett down dere to Leggett's Mill Pond.
A'ter freedom 'clare, uh lady from de north come dere en Miss
Leggett send we chillun to school to dat lady up on de hill
dere in de woods. No, honey, yuh ain' ne'er see no bresh tent

Code No.
Project, 1885-(1)
Prepared by Annie Ruth Davis
Place, Marion, S.C.
Date, June 21, 1937

No. Words_____
Reduced from____words
Rewritten by_____

Page 4.

60

'bout heah dis day en time. Dis jes de way it wuz make.
Dey dig four big holes en put postes in aw four corner
'bout lak uh room. Den dey lay log 'cross de top uv dat
en kiver it aw o'er wid bresh (brush) dat dey break outer
de woods. Ne'er hab none uv de side shet up. En dey haul
log dere en roll em under dat bresh tent fa we chillun to
set on. Oh, de teacher'ud hab uh big box fa her stand jes
lak uh preacher. Eve'ybody dat go to school dere hab one
uv dem t'ing call slate dat yuh ne'er hadder do nuthin but
jes wash it offen. En dey hab dese ole l'arnin' book wha'
yuh call Websters."

"My white folks al'ays wuz good to me, honey. Ne'er
didn't hab to/no field work in aw me life. When I stay
dere wid Miss Leggett, I hadder pick up little chip 'bout
de yard when I fust come home from school en den I hadder
go 'way up in de big field en drib de turkey/up. We didn't
find dat no hard t'ing to do lak de peoples talk lak it
sumptin hard to do dese days. We wuz l'arnt to work en
didn't mind it neither. Al'ays minded to us own business."

"Oh, gourds wuz de t'ing in dem days. Dey wuz wha' de
peoples hab to drink outer en wash dey hominy en rice in aw
de time. Dey wuz de bestest kind uv bowl fa we chillun to
eat corn bread en clabber outer. Peoples dis day en time
don' hab no sech crockery lak de people use'er hab. Honey,
dey hab de prettiest little clay bowls den."

Code No.
Project, 1885-(1)
Prepared by Annie Ruth Davis
Place, Marion, S.C.
Date, June 21, 1937

No. Words_____
Reduced from____words
Rewritten by

61

Page 5.

"Annuder t'ing de peoples do den dat yuh ain' ne'er hear 'bout nobody doing dese days, dey al'ays boil sumptin fa dey cows to eat lak peas en corn in uh big ole black pot somewhey dere in de back lot. Cose it wuz jes half cooked, but dey sho' done dat. Nobody ne'er t'ought 'bout not cookin' fa dey cow den."

"Dat wuz sho' uh different day from dis, honey. De little chillun wuz jes uz foolish den cause de peoples ne'er tell dem 'bout nuthin tall in dat day en time. Aw dese little chillun 'bout heah dese days don' hab no shame 'bout em no whey. Dey hab head full uv eve'yt'ing, honey, aw sorta grown people knowings."

Source: Maggie Black, ex-slave, age 79, Marion, S.C.
        Personal interview, June 1937.

FOLK-LORE: EX-SLAVES

"I was born in Laurens County, S. C., at the
'brick house', which is close to Newberry County line, and my
master was Dr. Felix Calmes. The old brick house is still there.
My daddy was Joe Grazier and my mammy, Nellie Grazier.

"We had a pretty good house to live in in slavery
time, and some fair things to eat, but never was paid any money.
We had plenty to eat like fat meat, turnips, cabbages, cornbread, milk and pot-liquor. Master sent his corn and apples,
and his peaches to old man Scruggs at Helena, near Newberry,
to have him make his whiskey, brandy, and wine for him. Old
man Scruggs was good at that business. The men hunted some,
squirrels, rabbits, possums, and birds.

"In the winter time I didn't have much clothes,
and no shoes. At nights I carded and spinned on the mistress's
wheels, helping my mammy. Then we got old woman Wilson to weave
for us.

" Master had a big plantation of several farms,
near about 1,000 acres or more. It was said he had once 250
slaves on his places, counting children and all. His overseers
had to whip the slaves, master told them to, and told them to
whip them hard. Master Calms was most always mean to us. He
got mad spells and whip like the mischief. He all the time
whipping me 'cause I wouldn't work like he wanted. I worked in
the big house, washed, ironed, cleaned up, and was nurse in the
house when war was going on.

"We didn't have a chance to learn to read and write, and master said if he caught any of his slaves trying to learn he would 'skin them alive'.

"There was a church in the neighborhood on Dr. Blackburn's place, but we didn't get to go to it much. I was 17 years old when I joined the church. I joined because the rest of the girls joined. I think everybody ought to join the church.

"On Saturday afternoons the slaves had to work, and all day Sunday, too, if master wanted them. On Christmas Day we was give liquor to get drunk on, but didn't have no dinner.

"When I was sick old Dr. P. B. Ruff attended me. Old Dr. Calmes, I 'member, traveled on a horse, with saddle-bag behind him, and made his own medicines. He made pills from cornbread.

"I saw many slaves sold on the block - saw mammy with little infant taken away from her baby and sent away. I saw families separated from each other, some going to one white master and some to another.

"I married at 14 years old to Arthur Bluford. We had 10 children. I now have about 8 grandchildren and about 7 or 8 great-grandchildren. I was married in the town of Newberry at the white folk's Methodist church, by a colored preacher named Rev. Geo. De Walt.

"When freedom come, they left and hired out to other people, but I stayed and was hired out to a man who tried to whip me, but I ran away. Dat was after I married and had little baby. I told my mammy to look after my little baby 'cause I was gone.

I stayed away two years 'till after Dr. Calmes and his family

moved to Mississippi."

SOURCE: Gordon Bluford (92), Newberry, S. C.
          Interviewer: G. Leland Summer, 1707 Lindsey St.,
                Newberry, S. C.

SAMUEL BOULWARE

EX-SLAVE 82 YEARS OLD.

Samuel Boulware's only home is one basement room, in the home
of colored friends, for which no rent charges are made. He is old and
feeble and has poor eyesight, yet, he is self-supporting by doing light
odd jobs, mostly for white people. He has never married, hence no depend-
ents whatever. One of the members of the house, in which Samuel lives,
told him someone on the front porch wanted to talk with him. -

From his dingy basement room he slowly mounted the steps and
came toward the front door with an irregular shamble. One seeing his
approach would naturally be of the opinion, that this old darkey was
certainly nearing the hundred year mark. Apparently Father Time had almost caught up with him; he had been caught in the winds of affliction
and now he was tottering along with a bent and twisted frame, which for
many years in the past, housed a veritable physical giant. The winds of
82 years had blown over him and now he was calmly and humbly approaching
the end of his days. Humility was his attitude, a characteristic purely
attributable to the genuine and old-fashion southern Negro. He slid into
a nearby chair and began talking in a plain conversational way.

"Dis is a mighty hot day white folks but you knows dis is July
and us gits de hot days in dis month. De older I gits de more I feels de
hot and de cold. I has been a strong, hard working man most all my life
and if it wasn't for dis rheumatism I has in my right leg, I could work
hard every day now.

"Does I 'member much 'bout slavery times? Well, dere is no way
for me to disremember, unless I die. My mammy and me b'long to Doctor

Hunter, some called him Major Hunter. When I was a small boy, I lived wid my mammy on de Hunter plantation. After freedom, I took de name of my daddy, who was a Boulware. He b'long to Reuben Boulware, who had a plantation two and one-half miles from Ridgeway, S. C., on de road dat leads to Longtown. My mistress' name was Effie. She and marster had four sons, no girls a-tall. George, Abram, Willie, and Henry, was their names. They was fine boys, 'cause they was raised by Mistress Effie's own hands. She was a good woman and done things 'zackly right 'round de plantation. Us slaves loved her, 'cause she said kind and soft words to us. Many times I's seen her pat de little niggers on de head, smile and say nice words to them. Boss, kind treatment done good then and it sho' does good dis present day; don't you think I's right 'bout dat? Marster had a bad temper. When he git mad, he walk fast, dis way and dat way, and when he stop, would say terrible cuss words. When de mistress heard them bad words, she would bow her pretty head and walk 'way kinda sad lak. It hurt us slaves to see de mistress sad, 'cause us wanted to see her smilin' and happy all de time.

"My mammy worked hard in de field every day and as I was just a small boy, I toted water to de hands in de field and fetched wood into de kitchen to cook wid. Mammy was de mother of twelve chillun; three of them die when they was babies. I's de oldest of de twelve and has done more hard work than de rest. I had five brothers and all of them is dead, 'cept one dat lives in Savannah, Georgia. I has four sisters, one living in Charleston, one in New York City, one in Ithaca, N. Y., and one in Fairfield County, dis State.

"Does my folks help me along any? No sir, they sho' don't. I

gits nothin' from them, and I don't expect nothin' neither. Boss, a
nigger's kinfolks is worse than a stranger to them; they thinks and
acts for theirselves and no one else. I knows I's a nigger and I tries
to know my place. If white folks had drapped us long time ago, us would
now be next to de rovin' beasts of de woods. Slavery was hard I knows
but it had to be, it seem lak. They tells me they eats each other in
Africa. Us don't do dat and you knows dat is a heap to us.

"Us had plenty to eat in slavery time. It wasn't de best but
it filled us up and give us strength 'nough to work. Marster would buy
a years rations on de first of every year and when he git it, he would
have some cooked and would set down and eat a meal of it. He would tell
us it didn't hurt him, so it won't hurt us. Dats de kind of food us
slaves had to eat all de year. Of course, us got a heap of vegetables
and fruits in de summer season, but sich as dat didn't do to work on,
in de long summer days.

"Marster was good, in a way, to his slaves but dat overseer
of his name John Parker, was mean to us sometimes. He was good to some
and bad to others. He strung us up when he done de whippin'. My mammy
got many whippin's on 'count of her short temper. When she got mad, she
would talk back to de overseer, and dat would make him madder than anything else she could do.

"Marster had over twenty grown slaves all de time. He bought
and sold them whenever he wanted to. It was sad times to see mother and
chillun separated. I's seen de slave speculator cut de little nigger
chillun with keen leather whips, 'cause they'd cry and run after de wagon
dat was takin' their mammies away after they was sold.

"De overseer was poor white folks, if dats what you is askin'

'bout, and dat is one thing dat made him so hard on de slaves of de
plantation. All de overseers I knowed 'bout was poor white folks;
they was white folks in de neighborhood dat wasn't able to own slaves.
All dis class of people was called by us niggers, poor white folks.

"Us slaves had no schoolin', 'cause dere was no teacher and
school nigh our plantation. I has learnt to read a little since I got
grown. Spelling come to me natural. I can spell most any word I hears,
old as I is.

"Marster and mistress was Baptist in 'ligious faith, and b'long
to Concord Baptist Church. Us slaves was allowed to 'tend dat church, too.
Us set up in de gallery and jined in de singin' every Sunday. Us slaves
could jine Concord Church but Doctor Durham, who was de preacher, would
take de slaves in another room from de white folks, and git their 'fessions,
then he would jine them to de church.

"My daddy was a slave on Reuben Boulware's plantation, 'bout two
miles from Marster Hunter's place. He would git a pass to come to see mammy
once every week. If he come more than dat he would have to skeedaddle through
de woods and fields from de patrollers. If they ketched him widout a pass,
he was sho' in for a skin crackin' whippin'. He knowed all dat but he would
slip to see mammy anyhow, whippin' or not.

"Most them there patrollers was poor white folks, I believes.
Rich folks stay in their house at night, 'less they has some sort of big
frolic amongst theirselves. Poor white folks had to hustle 'round to make
a living, so, they hired out theirselves to slave owners and rode de roads
at night and whipped niggers if they ketched any off their plantation widout

a pass. I has found dat if you gives to some poor folks, white or black, something a little better than they is used to, they is sho' gwine to think too high of theirselves soon, dats right. I sho' believes dat, as much as I believes I's setting in dis chair talkin' to you.

"I 'members lak yesterday, de Yankees comin' 'long. Marster tried to hide the best stuff on de plantation but some of de slaves dat helped him hide it, showed de Yankee soldiers just where it was, when they come dere. They say: 'Here is de stuff, hid here, 'cause us put it dere.' Then de soldiers went straight to de place where de valuables was hid and dug them out and took them, it sho' set old marster down. Us slaves was sorry dat day for marster and mistress. They was gittin' old, and now they had lost all they had, and more that dat, they knowed their slaves was set free. De soldiers took all de good hosses, fat cattle, chickens, de meat in de smoke house, and then burnt all empty houses. They left de ones dat folks lived in. De Yankees 'pear to me, to be lookin' for things to eat, more than anything else.

"Does I believe in 'ligion? Dat is all us has in dis world to live by and it's gwine to be de onliest thing to die wid. Belief in God and a 'umble spirit is how I's tryin' to live these days. I was christened fust a Methodist, but when I growed up, I jine de Presbyterian Church and has 'mained a member of dat church every since.

"Thank God I's had 'nough sense not to believe in haunts and sich things. I has 'possum hunt at night by myself in graveyards and I ain't seen one yet. My mammy say she see haunts pass her wid no heads but these old eyes has never seen anything lak dat. If you has done somebody a terrible wrong, then I believes dat person when they die, will 'pear to you on 'count of dat."

Project 1885-1
Folklore
Spartanburg, Dist.4
Feb. 7, 1938

Edited by:
Elmer Turnage

70

390027

REMINISCENCES: THE RED SHIRTS   Boyd

"The Red Shirts had a big parade and barbecue in Spartanburg.
They met at the courthouse. There were about 500 Red Shirts, besides
others who made up a big crowd. I remember four leaders who came from
Union County. One of the companies was led by Squire Gilliam Jeter,
and one by Squire Bill Lyles. The company from the city was led by
Capt. James Douglass, and 'Buck' Kelley from Pea Ridge was there with
his company.

"Everything drilled in Spartanburg that day. The speakers of
the day from Union were Squire Jeter and Capt. Douglass. While they
were speaking, old Squire George Tucker from lower Fish Dam came with
his company. Mr. Harrison Sartor, father of Will Sartor, was one of
the captains. We saw Gen. Wade Hampton and old man Ben Tillman there.

"About this time I was bound out to Mr. Jim Gregory, a blacksmith. The wealthy land lords bought negroes. Mr. Jim Gregory was the
blacksmith for old Johnny Meador and Aunt Polly, his wife. He told me
that Uncle Johnny bought a man, Heath, for $3,500. He also bought
Heath's wife, Morrow, for Aunt Polly, but I don't know what he paid.
The Meador house is just this side of Simstown. Aunt Polly's father,
Triplett Meador, built that mansion. The brick were made in a home
kiln which was near the house. Aunt Polly was a little girl when the
house was built. While the brick for the sitting-room fireplace were
still wet, he made little Polly step on each one of them to make the
impression of her feet. So those foot prints in that fireplace are
Aunt Polly's when she was five years old. She grew up there and married,
and lived there until her death.

"Miss Ida Knight's house (formerly the Sims house) was built not later than 1840. (Dr.) Thompson lived there first. Dr. Billy Sims married Dr. Thompson's sister, Miss Patsy, and that is how the house got into the Sims family. The old post office was known as Simstown, and I believe it was up near the Nat Gist mansion. Simstown was the name for the river community for years, because the Sims settled there and they were equally or more prominent than the Thompsons and Gists in that community. All the Sims men were country doctors.

"To this community at the close of the Confederate War, came old man Ogle Tate, his wife, and Ben Shell, as refugees, fleeing from the Yankees. When they came into the community, Nat Gist gave them a nice house to live in on his plantation.

"Mr. Gregory got all the sheet iron used on the Meador and Gist plantations, and also on the Sims and Thompson plantations. Plows were made in his blacksmith shop from 10 inch sheet iron. The sheet was heated and beaten into shape with his hammer. After cooling, the tools could be shappened. Horse and mule shoes were made from slender iron rods, bought for that purpose. They were called 'slats', and this grade of iron was known as 'slat iron'. The shoe was moulded while hot, and beaten into the correct shape to fit the animal's foot. Those old shoes fit much better than the store-bought ones of more recent days. The horseshoe nails were made there, too. In fact, every farm implement of iron was made from flat or sheet iron.

"I spun the first pants that I wore. Ma sewed them for me, and wove and finished them with her hands. She made the thread that they were sewed with by hand on the loom. I made cloth for all my shirts. I wore home-made cotton underwear in summer and winter, for we were poor. Of course my winter clothes were heavier.

"We raised some sheep, and the winter woolens were made from
the wool sheared from the sheep every May. Wool was taken to the factory at Bivensville and there made into yarn. Often, cotton was swap-
ped for yarn to warp at home. Then ma ran it off on spools for her
loom. 'Sleigh hammers' were made from cane gotten off the creek banks
and bottoms.

"Aunt Polly Meador had no patrollers on her place. She would
not allow one there, for she did her own patrolling with her own whip
and two bull dogs. She never had an overseer on her place, either.
Neither did she let Uncle Johnny do the whipping. Those two dogs held
them and she did her own whipping. One night she went to the quarter
and found old 'Bill Pea Legs' there after one of her negro women. He
crawled under the bed when he heard Aunt Polly coming. Those dogs
pulled old 'Pea Legs' out and she gave him a whipping that he never
forgot. She whipped the woman, also.

"Morg was Morrow's nickname. Morg used to sit on the meat
block and cut the meat for Aunt Polly to give out. Morg would eat her
three pounds of raw meat right there. Uncle Johnny asked her what she
would do all the week without any meat. She said that she would take
the skin and grease her mouth every morning; then go on to the field
or house and do her work, and wait until the next Saturday for more.

"I do not know how old I am, but I well remember when Wheeler's
men came to the plantation. They tore up everything. We heard that
they were coming, so we dug holes and buried the meat and everything
we could. We hid them so well that we could never find some of them
ourselves. Wheeler and 36 men stopped on the Dick Jeter place. I
think that was in 1864. The Jeter place touched Miss Polly's plantation. The Jeter place was right near Neal Shoals on Broad River. Mr.
Jeter had the biggest gin house in the entire township. Old Mr. Dick

was at home because he was too old to go to the war. Pa was still in
the war then, of course. Ma and I and one of the other children and
a few darkies were at our home.

"We saw Wheeler and his men when they stopped at that gin house.
They began to ransack immediately. Wheeler gave some orders to his men
and galloped off towards our house. The negroes ran but ma and I
stayed in the house. Wheeler rode up in front of the door and spoke to
my mother. He said that he had to feed his men and horses and asked
her where the corn was. She told him that the gin house and the crib
which contained the corn did not belong to her, so she could not give
him the keys. At that he ordered his men to remove a log from the crib.
By this means they broke into the crib and got all the corn. They
then ransacked the house and took everything there was to eat. They
tore out the big cog wheel in the gin and camped in it for the night.
Next morning they set fire to the gin and then gallpped away. Soon
Mr. Jeter's big gin had gone up in flames. They took all of our corn
and all of the fodder, 200 bundles that we had in the barn, away with
them.

Source: Mr. John Boyd, County Home, Union, R.F.D.
        Interviewer: Caldwell Sims, Union,S.C. 1/26/38

Project 1885-1
FOLKLORE
Spartanburg Dist.4
May 24, 1937

Edited by:
Elmer Turnage

STORIES FROM EX-SLAVES

"I was born in Newberry County, near the Laurens County line, above Little River. Me and my mother belonged to the Workman family. Afterwards, I belonged to Madison Workman. He was a good man to his slaves. My work was around the house and home. I was too young to work in the fields until after the war.

"I can't remember much about them times. I married there and soon after come to town and lived, where I have worked ever since. I do washing and other work.

"On the farm, the old folks had to cook outdoors, or in a kitchen away off from the house. They had wide fireplaces where they put their pots to cook the meals.

"I remember the old Little River Presbyterian Church where people would go on Sundays. They would go in the mornings, and again in the afternoons and have preaching."

Source: Jane Bradley (80), Newberry, S.C.
        Interviewer: G.L. Summer, Newberry, S.C. May 17, 1937

Project #1655
W. W. Dixon
Winnsboro, S. C.

ANDY BRICE

EX-SLAVE 81 YEARS OLD.

Andy Brice lives with his wife and two small children, about twelve miles east of Ridgeway, S. C., in a two-room frame building, chimney in the center. The house is set in a little cluster of pines one hundred and fifty yards north of state highway #34. Andy, since the amputation of his right leg five years ago, has done no work and is too old to learn a trade. He has a regular beggar's route including the towns of Ridgeway, Winnsboro, Woodward, and Blackstock. His amiability and good nature enable him to go home after each trip with a little money and a pack of miscellaneous gifts from white friends.

"Howdy Cap'in! I come to Winnsboro dis mornin' from way 'cross Wateree, where I live now 'mongst de bull-frogs and skeeters. Seem lak they just sing de whole night thru: 'De bull-frog on de bank, and de skeeter in de pool.' Then de skeeter sail 'round my face wid de tra la, la la la, la la la part of dat old song you is heard, maybe many times.

"I see a spit-box over dere. By chance, have you got any 'bacco? Make me more glib if I can chew and spit; then I 'members more and better de things done past and gone.

"I was a slave of Mistress Jane. Her was a daughter of old Marster William Brice. Her marry Henry Younge and mammy was give to Marse Henry and Miss Jane.

"My pappy name Tony. Mammy name Sallie. You is seen her a many a day. Marse Henry got kilt in de war. His tombstone and Mistress Jane's tombstone am in Concord Cemetery. They left two chillun, Miss Kittie and Miss Maggie. They both marry a Caldwell; same name but no kin. Miss Kittie marry Marse Joe

Caldwell and move to Texas. Miss Maggie marry Marse Camel Caldwell and move to North Carolina.

"My pappy die durin' de war. After freedom, mammy marry a ugly, no 'count nigger name Mills Douglas. She had one child by him, name Janie. My mammy name her dat out of memory and love for old mistress, in slavery time. I run away from de home of my step-pappy and got work wid Major Thomas Brice. I work for him 'til I become a full grown man and come to be de driver of de four-hoss wagon.

"One day I see Marse Thomas a twistin' de ears on a fiddle and rosinin' de bow. Then he pull dat bow 'cross de belly of dat fiddle. Sumpin' bust loose in me and sing all thru my head and tingle in my fingers. I make up my mind, right then and dere, to save and buy me a fiddle. I got one dat Christmas, bless God! I learn and been playin' de fiddle ever since. I pat one foot while I playin'. I kept on playin' and pattin' dat foot for thirty years. I lose dat foot in a smash up wid a highway accident but I play de old tunes on dat fiddle at night, dat foot seem to be dare at de end of dat leg (indicating) and pats just de same. Sometime I ketch myself lookin' down to see if it have come back and jined itself up to dat leg, from de very charm of de music I makin' wid de fiddle and de bow.

"I never was very popular wid my own color. They say behind my back, in '76, dat I's a white folks nigger. I wear a red shirt then, drink red liquor, play de fiddle at de 'lection box, and vote de white folks ticket. Who I marry? I marry Ellen Watson, as pretty a ginger cake nigger as ever fried a batter cake or rolled her arms up in a wash tub. How I git her? I never git her; dat fiddle got her. I play for all de white folks dances down at Cedar Shades, up at Blackstock. De money roll in when someone pass 'round de hat and say: 'De fiddler?' Ellen had more beaux 'round her than her could shake a stick at but de beau she lak best was de bow dat could draw music out of them five strings, and draw money into dat hat, dat jingle in my pocket de nex' day when I go to see her.

"I 'members very little 'bout de war, tho' I was a good size boy when de Yankees come. By instint, a nigger can make up his mind pretty quick 'bout de creed of white folks, whether they am buckra or whether they am not. Every Yankee I see had de stamp of poor white trash on them. They strutted 'round, big Ike fashion, a bustin' in rooms widout knockin', talkin' free to de white ladies, and familiar to de slave gals, ransackin' drawers, and runnin' deir bayonets into feather beds, and into de flower beds in de yards.

"What church I b'long to? None. Dat fiddle draws down from hebben all de sermons dat I understan'. I sings de hymns in de way I praise and glorify de Lord.

"Cotton pickin' was de biggest work I ever did, outside of drivin' a wagon and playin' de fiddle. Look at them fingers; they is supple. I carry two rows of cotton at a time. One week I pick, in a race wid others, over 300 pounds a day. Commencin' Monday, thru Friday night, I pick 1,562 pounds cotton seed. Dat make a bale weighin' 500 pounds, in de lint.

"Ellen and me have one child, Sallie Ann. Ellen 'joy herself; have a good time nussin' white folks chillun. Nussed you; she tell me 'bout it many time. 'Spect she mind you of it very often. I knows you couldn't git 'round dat woman; nobody could. De Lord took her home fifteen years ago and I marry a widow, Ida Belton, down on de Kershaw County side.

"You wants me to tell 'bout dat 'lection day at Woodward, in 1878? You wants to know de beginnin' and de end of it? Yes? Well, you couldn't wet dis old man's whistle wid a swallow of red liquor now? Couldn't you or

could you? Dis was de way of it: It was set for Tuesday. Monday I drive
de four-hoss wagon down to dis very town. Marse John McCrory and Marse Ed
Woodward come wid me. They was in a buggy. When us got here, us got twenty,
sixteen shooters and put them under de hay us have in de wagon. Bar rooms
was here. I had fetched my fiddle 'long and played in Marse Fred Habernick's
bar 'til dinner time. Us leave town 'bout four o'clock. Roads was bad but
us got home 'bout dark. Us put de guns in Marse Andy Mobley's store. Marse
Ed and me leave Marse John to sleep in de store and to take care of de guns.

"De nex' mornin', polls open in de little school house by de brick
church. I was dere on time, help to fix de table by de window and set de
ballot boxes on it. Voters could come to de window, put deir arms thru and
tuck de vote in a slit in de boxes. Dere was two supervisors, Marse Thomas
for de democrats and Uncle Jordan for de Radicals. Marse Thomas had a book
and a pencil, Uncle Jordan had de same.

"Joe Foster, big buckra nigger, want to vote a stranger. Marse
Thomas challenge dis vote. In them times colored preachers so 'furiate de
women, dat they would put on breeches and vote de 'publican radical ticket.
De stranger look lak a woman. Joe Foster 'spute Marse Thomas' word and Marse
Thomas knock him down wid de naked fist. Marse Irish Billy Brice, when him
see four or five hindred blacks crowdin' 'round Marse Thomas, he jump thru de
window from de inside. When he lit on de ground, pistol went off pow! One
nigger drop in his tracks. Sixteen men come from nowhere and sixteen, sixteen
shooters. Marse Thomas hold up his hand to them and say: 'Wait!' Him point
to de niggers and say: 'Git.' They start to runnin' 'cross de railroad, over
de hillside and never quit runnin' 'til they git half a mile away. De only
niggers left on dat ground was me, old Uncle Kantz, (you know de old mulatto,

club-foot nigger) well, me and him and Albert Gladney, de hurt nigger dat was shot thru de neck was de only niggers left. Dr. Tom Douglas took de ball out Albert's neck and de white folks put him in a wagon and sent him home. I drive de wagon. When I got back, de white boys was in de grave-yard gittin' names off de tombstones to fill out de talley sheets, dere was so many votes in de box for de Hampton ticket, they had to vote de dead. I 'spect dat was one resurrection day all over South Carolina."

Project 1885-1
Folklore
Spartanburg, Dist.4
Nov. 10, 1937

390367

Edited by:
Elmer Turnage   80

STORIES FROM EX-SLAVES

"I is gwine over to Tosch to see Maria. Everybody know
Maria. She go by Rice -- Maria Rice. She sont fer me to cure her
misery. First, I went from my home in lower Cross Keys, across de
Enoree, to see Maria. When I reached dar whar she stay, dey tell me
dat her daughter over to Tosch. Done come and got her.

"A kind friend dat de Lawd put in my path fetched me back
across de Enoree and over to Tosch to Maria's gal's house. I is
gwine straight over dar and lay my hand on Maria and rid her of dat
misery dat she sont word was ailing her all dis spring. Don't make
no diff'uns whar you hurts -- woman, man or suckling babe -- if you
believes in de holler of my hand, it'll ease you, allus do it. De
Bible say so, dat's why it be true. Ain't gwine to tell you nothing
but de truth and de whole truth, so help me Jesus. Gone 65 years,
I is been born agin dat long; right over in Padgett's Creek church,
de white folks' church, dat's whar de Lawd tuck my sins away and
washed me clean agin wid His blood. Dat's why I allus sticks to de
truth, I does.

"Dey all 'lows dat I is gwine on 89, and I has facts to believe it am true. I 'longed to Marse Jesse Briggs. Did you know dat
it was two Jesse Briggs? Yes sir, sho was two Jesse Briggses.

"What I gwine to relate to you is true, but in respect to
my old Marse, and in de case dat dem what reads dat book won't
understand, you needs not to write dis statement down. My marster
was called 'Black Jesse', but de reason fer dat was to keep him from
gitting mixed up wid de other Jesse. Dat is de secret of de thing.

Now dat's jes' fer your own light and knowledge, and not to be
wrote down. He was de blacksmith fer all de Cross Keys section,
and fer dat very thing he got de name by everybody, 'Black Jesse'.
I allus 'longed to dat man and he was de kindest man what de
countryside had knowledge of.

      "In Union County is whar I was born and raised, and it's
whar I is gwine to be buried. Ain't never left de county but once
in my life, and if de Lawd see fitten, I ain't gwine to leave it
no mo', 'cept to reach de Promise Land. Lawd! Lawd! De Promise Land,
dat's whar I is gwine when I leaves Union County. Dey carried me
a hundred miles to cure a sick woman, onliest time I ever left
Union County. I loves it and I is fit throughout and enduring de
time dem Yankees tried to git de county, to save it. What is I
gwine to leave it fer? Mr. Perrin and all de white folks is good to
me since my marse done gone and left his earthly home. And he is
waiting up dar wid Missie to see me agin. Dat I is sho of.

      "Listen brother, de Lawd is setting on His throne in Glory.
He hear every word dat I gwine to tell you. Folks fergits dat when
dey talks real often sometimes, don't dey? I put my hand on any 'flux'
man or woman and removes de pain, if dey have faith in my hand. I
don't tell nothing but de truth. I was born on Gist Briggs' plantation
in Union County, in de lower section of Cross Keys. Marse Sexton and
all dem good folks in lower Keys says dat I sho is 88. Give my name
right flat, it's George Briggs; giving it round, it like dis, George
McDuffie Briggs. My papa's name was Ike Wilburn, and my mother's
name was Margaret Briggs. Pa 'longed to Marse Lige Wilburn. Mama
'longed to Jesse (Black Jesse) Briggs. Dey both born and raised in
Union County. Dese was my brothers and sisters, coming in de order
dey was born to my parents in: Charlie, Dave, Aaron, Tom, Noah,

Charlotte, Polly, Fannie, Mattie, Horace, Cassie. I'm de oldest, and
Cassie and me lives in Union County. Fannie and Mattie lives in Ashe-
ville, and de rest is done journeyed to de Promise Land. Yes Lawd, to
de Promise Land.

"Marse and Missus was good to us all. Missus name was Nancy.
She die early and her grave is in Cross Keys at de Briggs graveyard.
Be still! Lemme git my mind together so dat I don't git mixed up and
can git you de Briggses together. Here 'tis: Cheney and Lucindy,
Lucindy married a Floyd from Spartanburg, and de Floyds lived at de
Burn't Factory. Cheney Briggs had a son, Henry Briggs.

"Not so fast, fer I'se gwine to start way back, dat time
when us was lil' darky boys way back in slavery. We started to work
wid de marster's mules and hosses. When us was real little, we played
hoss. Befo' Cheney Briggs went to Arkansas he was our play hoss. His
brother, Henry, was de wagoner and I was de mule. Henry was little
and he rid our backs sometimes. Henry rid old man Sam, sometimes, and
old man Sam jes' holler and haw haw at us chilluns. Dis was in sech
early childhood dat it is not so I can 'zactly map out de exact age
us was den; anyway, from dis we rid de gentle hosses and mules and
larn't how to feed dem. Every word dat I tells you is de truth, and
I is got to meet dat word somewhars else; and fer dat reason, de
truth is all dat dis old man ever tells.

"In dat day we lived in a log cabin or house. Sometimes us
never had nothing to do. Our house had only one room, but some of de
houses had two rooms. Our'n had a winder, a do', and a common fireplace. Now dey makes a fireplace to scare de wood away. In old days
dey made fireplaces to take care of de chilluns in de cold weather.
It warm de whole house, 'cause it was so big and dar was plenty wood.

Wood wasn't no problem den, and it ain't no problem yet out in de
lower Keys. In town it is, and I ain't guessing. I done seed so.

"I sho can histronize de Confederates. I come along wid
de Secession flag and de musterings. I careful to live at home and
please de Marse. In de war, I'se mo' dan careful and I stick close
to him and please him, and he mo' dan good. Us did not git mobbed
up like lots of dem did.

"When Tice Myers' chilluns was born, he had a house built
wid a up-stairs. But never no stage coach stopped dar as I ever heard
tell about, and I done saw 75 years at Padgett's Creek.

"Way 'tis, from de bundle of de heart, de tongue speaketh.
Been in service reg'lar since Monday. I went to Neal Greege's house
but she wasn't dar. I is speaking 'bout Ria (Maria Rice). She done
gone to town. At de highway, de Lawd prepared a friend to carry me
to Union, and when I got dar I take and lay hands on Ria Rice. She
laying down and suffering, and I sot down and laid my hand on her. We
never say nothing, jes' pray. She be real quiet, and atter while,
she riz up and take a breath. She kept on a setting up fer so long
dat her husband make her lay back down fer fear dat she git worser.
I stay dar all through de night and she sleep sound and wake up dis
morning feeling like a new woman.

"Befo' breakfast, here is de words of praise I lifted to
de Lawd, over dar on Tosch. You set down de coser (chorus): 'First
to de graveyard; den to de Jedgement bar!' Is you got dat verser?
Den git dis: 'All de deacons got to go; all de members got to go;
all de sinners got to go.' Mo' 'longs to it, but dat's all I takes
when I is praising Him fer relieving pain through me. (He sings each
line five times, He takes off his hat; bows; holds his hands over his
head, and closes his eyes while singing. His hair is snow white.)

"Lawd, help me dis morning! Here's another first line to one of our songs: 'All dem preachers got to go'.

"Nehemiah, when he wid de king, de king axed him to reveal de wall whar his father was buried. Nehemiah did what de king had done axed him. I 'tends Galilee Baptist church in lower Cross Keys; and at Sedalia, I goes to New Hope Methodist church, but I don't know nothing else but Baptist. We peoples is barrence (barren of the Holy Spirit), but not God; He, Hisself, is born of God, and all is of de same source and by dat I means de Spirit. All has to be born of de Spirit to become chilluns of God. Romans, Chap.6, 'lows something like dis: 'He dat is dead in sin, how is it dat he can continue in sin?' Dat tell us dat every man, white or black, is de child of God. And it is Christ dat is buried in baptism, and we shall be buried in like manner. If Christ did not rise, den our preaching is in vain. And if we is not born agin, why den we is lost and our preaching is in vain.

"In picking up de New Testament, consider all dat you hear me arguing and saying is from a gift and not from edication. Romans 6, 'lows: 'Speak plain words, not round words, kaise all de round words is fer dem dat is edicated.' Jacob had twelve sons. Dey went and bundled up deir wheat, and eleven bundles bowed to de one. Dat Joseph's bundle what he done up. Other brothers up and got and sold Joseph into captivity to de Egyptians. Dat throw'd Jacob to send Reuben to Egypt. Den dey bowed to Jacob and his sons. It run on and on till dey all had to go to Egypt, and all of dem had to live under Joseph.

"When I was a little shaver and come to myself, I was sleeping in a corded bed. (He scratched his head) I jes' studying fer a minute; can't 'zactly identify my grandpa, but I can identify

my grandma. We all raised on de same place together. She name Cindy

Briggs, but dey call her Cina kaise dar was so many Cindys 'round

dar. One thing I does 'member 'bout her, if she tote me, she sho

to whip me. I was raised strict.

"All my life I is stayed in de fur (far) end of Union

County whar it borders Laurens, wid de Enoree dividing de two coun-

ties. It is right dar dat I is plowed and hoed and raised my craps

fer de past 75 years, I reckons. Lawd have mercy! No, I doesn't re-

calls de names of none of dem mules. Dat's so fur back dat I is jes'

done forgot, dat's all. But I does recall 'fur back' things de best,

sometimes. Listen good now. When I got big and couldn't play 'round

at chillun's doings, I started to platting cornshucks and things fer

making hoss and mule collars, and scouring-brooms and shoulder-mats.

I cut hickory poles and make handles out of dem fer de brooms. Marse

had hides tanned, and us make buggy whips, wagon whips, shoe strings,

saddle strings and sech as dat out of our home-tanned leather. All

de galluses dat was wo' in dem days was made by de darkies.

"White oak and hickory was split to cure, and we made fish

baskets, feed baskets, wood baskets, sewing baskets and all kinds of

baskets fer de Missus. All de chair bottoms of straight chairs was

made from white oak splits, and de straight chairs was made in de

shop. You made a scouring brush like dis: (He put his hands together

to show how the splits were held) By splitting a width of narrow

splits, keep on till you lay a entire layer of splits; turn dis way;

den dat way, and den bind together and dat hold dem like you want dem

to stay. Last, you work in a pole as long as you want it fer de

handle, and bind it tight and tie wid de purtiest knots.

"I git money fer platting galluses and making boot strings
and other little things. Allus first, I desires to be well qualified
wid what I does. I is gwine to be qualified wid everything dat I
does, iffen I does it fer money or no. Dat's de reason white people
has allus give me words of encouragement.

"Now I gwine to sing a song fer Miss Polly, kaise she de
grand-daughter of de late Sheriff Long, and I goes to see her grandma at de Keys (Cross Keys House). Dar she come now.

"How is you dis morning, Miss Polly? De Lawd sho does
shower you, Miss Polly, and dat's de reason I is gwine to sing fer
you dis morning. You'll be able to tell Mr. Jimmie (her father) dat
Uncle George sing fer you, 'Jesus Listening All De Day Long'.

"Jesus listening all de day long to hear some sinner pray.
De winding sheet to wrop (wrap) dis body in,
De coffin to hold you fast;
Pass through death's iron do'.
Come ye dat love de Lawd and let your joy be know'd;
Dis iron gate you must pass through, if you gwine to be
Born agin."

He sang these lines over three times and then bowing, said:
"Ain't it glory dat we can live whar de Lawd can use us? Dat's power.
A strong man entereth in; a weak man cometh out. Dat represent Christ
gwine into your heart.

"Sho I can remember when dey had de mustering grounds at de
Keys. Dar dey mustered and den dey turn't in and practiced drilling
dem soldiers till dey larn't how to march and to shoot de Yankees.
Drilling, dat's de proper word, not practice. I knows, if I ain't
ed'icated. Dey signed me to go to de 16th regiment, but I never

reached de North. When us got to Charleston, us turn't around and de
bosses fetched us right back to Union through Columbia. Us heard dat
Sherman was coming, fetching fire along 'hind him.

"Don't know nothing 'bout no militia to make no statement,
but it went on and turn't back. Another regiment had a barbecue
somewhars in Union County befo' it went off to war; might a been de
18th regiment, but I does not feel dat I can state on dat.

"My soul reaches from God's footstool up to his heavenly
home. I can histronize de poor white folks' wives and chilluns enduring de time of de Civil War fer you. When dese poor white men
went to de war, dey left deir little chillun and deir wives in de
hands of de darkies dat was kind and de rich wives of our marsters
to care fer. Us took de best care of dem poor white dat us could
under de circumstances dat prevailed.

"We was sont to Sullivan's Island, but befo' we reached
it, de Yankees done got it and we won't 'lowed to cross in '64. But
jes' de same, we was in service till dey give Capt. Franklin Bailey
'mission to fetch us home. Dar we had to git 'mission fer everything,
jes' as us niggers had to git 'mission to leave our marster's place
at home in Union County. Capt. Bailey come on back to Cross Keys
wid us under his protection, and we was under it fer de longest
time atter we done got home.

"Fer 65 years I been licensed as a preacher, and fer longer
dan dat I been a member of Padgett's Creek Baptist church. Mo' work
I does, mo' work I has to do. You know how to pray. Well, you does
not know how to make polish out of pinders.

"I ain't ed'icated yet, but even Lige what teaches school
out to de Keys (de big black school), dat big black buck dat teaches
de chilluns deir 'rithmetic; even he couldn't do dis here one.

A heap of ed'icated folks can't give it. Here it is: 'What's de biggest figger in de figger ten?'"

With his old black, rough and gnarled forefinger he drew on the table the figure 1. "Now you see dat? Dat's de figger 1. A naught ain't nothing by itself or multiplied by other naughts; but set it down in front of de figger 1, and it takes on de value 9. Dar you is got ten -- one and nine is ten. Dat naught becomes something. I is old, and I ain't had narry bit of schooling, but I likes to be close to de orchard, and I knows it's dar by de smell of it. Dat's de way I is when I gits along side ed'icated folks -- I knows dat dey is.

"It's like dat sum dem scholars couldn't git; standing alone dat naught ain't worth nothing, but set it up against dat which is of value and it takes on value. Set a naught ag'inst dat which is one and you has ten; set up another naught dar and you has a hundred. Now if somebody was to give me a note worth $10, and I found room to add another naught along side of de first; den dem two naughts what ain't worth nothing by deirselves gives de note de value of $99 if dey is sot along wid de one. Ed'icated folks calls dat raising de note. I is ig'nant and I calls dat robbery. And dat's like you and me. We is naughts and Christ is de One, and we ain't nothing till we carries de Spirit of de Lawd along wid us.

"On de pathway of life, may you allus keep Christ in front of you and you will never go wrong. De Lawd will den see fit to give you a soul dat will reach from His foot-stool here on earth to His dwelling place on high." He ended with a deep sob and good-bye.

Source: George Briggs (88), Union, S.C. RFD 2.
         Interviewer: Caldwell Sims, Union, S.C. 6/9/37.

Project 1885-1
FOLKLORE
Spartanburg Dist.4
July 20, 1937

390130

Edited by:
Elmer Turnage   89

STORIES FROM EX-SLAVES

"Some white men called in question today about de reigning governor enduring time of de Civil War. I knowed dat, and 'cides dat, I knowed him well. It was Governor 'Bill' as us called him.

"What you want to git, is history about muster grounds. Yes, it was on Jones Ferry Road, jest south of Cross Keys whar dey had what dey allus called de muster field. Now, Jones Ferry Road leads across Enoree River into Laurens County. Enoree River is de thing dat devides Union County from Laurens County, dat it is.

"Well as I remember, Mr. Bill Ray was in de mustering of de 18th Regiment. Billy, Robert, Sam and Miss Nancy was Mr. Alex's chilluns. Understand me, don't think dat Bob and Sam was in de Regiment ... satisfied Billy was, kaise he used to pass our house on horse back, coming from de Laurens side where he lived.

"Sixteen-year-old boys come in de same time dat I did. Course I ain't told all dat I knows, kaise dat wouldn't be proper. All I tell you, I wants it to be recognized. De better it's done, de better it'll help you.

"I goes from home and stays five days or more, and don't nothing happen to a thing at my home. I does fer de sick and de Lawd blesses me. He looks atter my things while I am away. He soon shows his presence atter I gits dar. He calls fer me and I feeds Him.

"Once had 26 biles (boils). Dat make me consider my disobedience against de Lawd. Den I went to Him in prayer. He told me Satan done got ahead of Him. Dat show me dat I done forgot to be particular. I got mo' 'ticular and pray mo' often, and in six weeks my biles had done all gone.

"Dar is times when I gits lost fer not knowing. I can't keep up, kaise I cannot read. Man in Sunday school reads and I hears. He read de olden Testament; den he read de new Testament. Dat my schooling. I 'clar unto you, I got by all my life by praying and thinking. I sho does think a lot. ('Uncle' George's facial and scalp muscles work so when he thinks, that his straw hat moves up and down.)

"When good man prays fer bad man, de Holy Ghost works on bad man's consciousness, and afo' he knows it, he's a-saying 'Lawd have Mercy' 'stead of 'G'dam', like all wicked folks says every day. He ---dat de Holy Ghost dat I still is speaking of-- jest penetrates de wicked man's consciousness widout him a-knowing it. Dat penetrating make de bad man say, 'Lawd have Mercy.' I hoes and I cuts sprouts, and den I plows. When you plows, mules is allus so aggravating dat dey gits you all ruffled up. Dat de devil a-working at you. Dat's all old mules is anyhow. I does not cuss, no-how, kaise it sho am wicked and I is had de Holy Spirit in my soul, now gone sixty-five years, since I jined Padgett Creek Church. When my old mule gits to de row's end, and he act mulish -- kaise dat's in him and he don't know nothing else to do -- I means to say either 'ha' or 'gee', and often since I jined Padgett Creek Church I finds myself saying 'Lawd have Mercy' 'stead of 'gee' or 'ha'. So you see dat de Lawd has command, whar-so-ever if I was wicked, Satan would.

"A child fo God allus will agree wid de Word of God. We mens dat claim to be leaders in de Kingdom, got to step up and sho folks what dey must do. Man learns right smart from Exodus 'bout how to lead. A male child was born to rule de world. Moses still de strongest impression dat we has as rulers. God gits His-self into de heads of men dat he wants to rule and He don't tell nobody else nothing 'bout it neither.

"Mr. Roosevelt de president and he sho looks atter de po' folks. He ain't no ig'nant man neither, kaise he got de light. Folks ain't a-gwine to drown him out neither wid dere wicked words 'gainst him, kaise he strive in de Lawd's name to do His will. Mr. Roosevelt got learning like I is from de throne of God. He may have education also, but if he is, he sho knows how to keep dem both jined together. Folks reads to me how he got crippled and how he washed in dem springs in Georgia, and dat keep him a-gwine right on anyhow. It ain't dem springs by deself, but it's God a dipping his hand down dar fer de President to git well. Oh yes, suh, I knows dat he twan't de president when he was a-washing, but dem de plans dat de Lawd had done already planned and you and me never know'd nothing 'bout all dat. You and me does not know what is planned up in sto' fer us in de future neither.

"I is a Baptist, and at Padgett's Creek we does not believe in no back-sliding. 'Once in de Spirit, allus in de Spirit'. A child of your'n is allus a child of your'n. Dat de way de Baptist teach -- once a child of God, allus God's child.

T'ain't no sech thing as drapping back. If you draps back, you ain't never been no child of de Lawd, and you never had no business being baptized. Christ was baptized in de waters of Jordan, won't (weren't) He? Well, He never drapped back, did He? He say we must follow in His footsteps, didn't He? Well, dar you is, and dat's all dar is to it..

"God gits in de heads of men to help de aged and de po' also. I never axes fer nothing, but when I sets around de courthouse and informs men as I been doing dis evening, de Lawd has dem to drap a nickle or a dime or a quarter in my hand but He never gits dem to a half of a dollar."

Source: George Briggs,(88) Rt.2, Union, S.C.
        Interviewer: Caldwell Sims, Union, S.C. (7/12/37)

Project 1885-1
FOLKLORE
Spartanburg Dist.4
July 12, 1937

390143

Edited by:
Elmer Turnage

93

STORIES FROM EX-SLAVES

"What-so-ever I can find! I traveling dat way over
73 years. If he ax de Lawd and have faith, he ken do; and
iffen he don't have no faith, by den he can't. When a man
comes along dat wants his own way, and he won't pay no
attention to de Lawd, by den de Lawd don't pay him no mind;
and so dat man jest keeps a-gwine on wid his way and he
don't never reach de Cross. Jesus say, 'deny yourself, pick
up de Cross and follow Me.'

"I see a man in de courthouse dis morning, and he
was like Nicodemus. Why dat man want to be resto'd back like
he was when he was jest 21 years old. I seed him setting
down dar in Mr. Perrin's office, and I knowed his troubles
when he 'low dat he done been to every doctor in town. De
trouble was, he never had no faith in de doctors and nobody
else. How could he have faith in Jesus when he never had
none in nothing else? Brother, you has to have faith in
your fellowman befo' you has faith in de Lawd. I don't know
how come, but dat's de way it is. My plan is working by
faith. Jesus say, 'Work widout faith ain't nothing; but
work wid faith'll move mountains'.

"Dat man told me he gwine give me a hundred dollars
if I rid him of misery. Dat show he never know nothing 'bout
faith.

"If Mr. Emslie Nicholson ax me to rid him of a
misery, I couldn't take no money from him, and he de richest
man in all Union County. Mr. Nicholson would know better dan
to offer me money, kaise he has faith. You know he's a good
'Presmuterian' (Presbyterian).

"Dey looks at de back of my head, and de hair on
it ain't rubbed against no college and fer dat reason dese
young negroes don't want me to preach. Dey wants to hear dat
man preach dat can read. Man dat can read can't understand
less'n some divine man guide him. I speak as my Teacher gives
it to me, dat's de Lawd. In so doing, I testify de word dat
no man can condemn. Dat is my plan of Salvation: to work by
faith widout price or purse, as de Lawd, my Teacher has
taught me.

"Dar was no church on our plantation when I was a
boy. All de Baptists went to Padgett's Creek, and all de
Methodist went to Quaker Church and Belmont. Padgett's Creek
had a section in de back of de church fer de slaves to sit.
Quaker Church and Belmont both had slaves' galleries. Dar
is a big book at Padgetts wid three pages of slaves' names
that was members. Mr. Claude Sparks read it to me last year.
All de darky members dead, but one, dat's me.

"Nobody never read de Bible to me when I was little.
It jest a gift of God dat teached to me through de Holy Ghost.
It's de Spirit of de One in Three dat gits into you, and dat's
de Holy Ghost or de Holy Spirit dat gives me my enlightment.

"If I can git to de do' of Padgett's Creek Church,
I can jest feel de Power of God. ('Uncle' George pats his
foot and softly cries at this point, and his face takes on
a calm and peaceful expression.)

"If you eats befo' you gits hongry, you never will
feast on dead air. I makes it a practice to feed my soul and
body befo' dey gits hongry. Even I does eat by myself, dis old
man take off his hat and ax de Lawd to bless his soul and body
in nourishment fer de future.

"I ain't never seed Mr. Lincoln, but from what I
learn't dey said dat God had placed in him de revelation to
give de plan dat he had fer every man. Dat plan fer every man
to worship under his own vine and fig tree. From dat, we
should of liked Mr. Lincoln.

"Dis here 'Dick Look-Up', No sir, I don't know him,
kaise I caught his name since I come on dis side of de river.
Mr. Perrin knows him, and I heard him say dat every time anybody ax him how old he is, he add on ten years. Dat's how come
dey got in de paper he a hundred and twenty-five years old.
Now me and Mr. Perrin doesn't speak unless we is obleeged to
know dat what we is gwine to say is de truth. Us is careful,
kaise us knows dat de Lawd am looking down from his throne,
and dat He is checking every word dat we says. Some folks does
not recall dat fact when dey speaks, or dey would be careful.

"I'll say it slow so dat you can catch it; I start
in time of de Confederate War. Wid dirt dug up out of de smoke-
house, water was run through it so us could get salt fer bread.

Hickory wood ashes was used fer soda. If we didn't have no
hickory wood, we burnt red corn cobs; and de ashes from dem
was used fer cooking soda.

"Molasses was made from watermelions in time of de
war. Dey was also made from May-apples or may-pops as some
call dem, and sometimes dey was made from persimmons and
from wheat brand. In Confederate days, Irish potato tops was
cooked fer vegetables. Blackberry leaves was ocassionally
used fer greens or fer seasoning lambs quarters.

"Dis way watermelion was done: Soak watermelion
twenty and four hours to de'self; strain off all juice and
put on fire to bile. When dey thickens dey bees good, Yes
sir, good, good,

"Wid may-pops: peel de outside green off, den bust
'em open and mash up together; strain juice off and cook thick.

" 'Simmons and wheat bran are mashed up together and
baked in water. Let set twenty and four hours and cook down
to molasses. Dat winds up dat part of it.

"Git plums and blackberries and de like of dat and
make up in Jelly, or can fer scarce times, dat's de way we
done den and folks does dat yet. Dese is some of de particular-
est things of de Confederate times dat I come back from
Sedalia to give you, dat's right. (This old negro, who had
already been interviewed by the writer, came a long way and
looked-up the author to tell him some incidents which he had
forgotten to tell in the first interview.) Some customs is
done went by now, but dey was practiced in Sedalia, and as to
whar dem was done fer off as Spartanburg, I cannot say.

"In Confederate time, all wimmens stayed close home and carded and spun all de day long. Dey wove all dere own clothes. Men at home, old men, made leather shoes and shoe strings and belts and galloses.

"Our darkies tried hard to be obedient to our master so dat we might obtain (keep) our pleasant home. Obedience makes it better dan sacrifice. I restes my minds dar."

Source: George Briggs (88), Rt.2, Union,S.C.
        Interviewed by: Caldwell Sims, Union, S.C. (7/7/37)

Code No.
Project, 1865-(1)
Prepared by Annie Ruth Davis
Place, Marion, S.C.
Date, January 27, 1938

No. ~~Words~~
Reduced from ____ words
Rewritten by
Page 1.

98

390010

JOSEPHINE BRISTOW
Ex-Slave, 73 Years

"Remembers de Confederate War, Miss. Yes,mam, I'm
supposed to be, if I can live to see February, bout 73
year old. What age Hester say she was? Dat what I had
thought from me en her conversation. Miss, I don' remember
a thing more bout de war den de soldiers comin through old
Massa's plantation en we chillun was 'fraid of dem en ran.
Knew dey was dressed in a different direction from us white
folks. All was in blue, you know, wid dem curious lookin
hats en dem brass buttons on dey bodies. No,mam, dey didn'
stop nowhe' bout us. Dey was ridin on horses en it seem like
dey was in a hurry gwine somewhe'. En dey didn' stop to old
Massa's house neither. No,mam, not to my knowin, dey didn'.
Well, we was livin out to de plantation, we calls it, en Massa
en Missus was livin up here to Marion. Mr. Ferdinand Gibson,
dat who been us Massa in slavery time en Miss Connie, dat what
we used to call her, was us Missus. To my knowin, dey didn'
have no chillun dey own, but dey sho had plenty colored people.
Yes,mam, seems like to my remembrance , my Massa ran bout 30
plantations en 'sides dat, he had a lot of servants right up
here to de big house, men en women."

"I was real small in dem days en far as I can remember,
we lived on de quarter dere to old Massa's plantation in de

Code No.
Project, 1885-(1)
Prepared by Annie Ruth Davis
Place, Marion, S.C.
Date, January 27, 1938

No. Words_____
Reduced from___words
Rewritten by   99
_____
Page 2.

country. Us little tots would go every mornin to a place up
on de hill, called de milk house, en get our milk 'tween meals
while de old folks was off workin. Oh, dey had a old woman to
see after we chillun en tend to us in de daytime. De old lady
dat looked after us, her name was Mary Novlin. Lord, Mr. Gibson,
he had big farms en my mother en father, dey worked on de farms.
Yes'um, my mother en father, I used to never wouldn' know when
dey come home in de evenin, it would be so late. De old lady,
she looked after every blessed thing for us all day long en
cooked for us right along wid de mindin. Well, she would boil
us corn meal hominy en give us dat mostly wid milk for breakfast. Den dey would have a big garden en she would boil peas
en give us a lot of soup like dat wid dis here oven bread. Oh,
dem what worked in de field, dey would catch dey meals when dey
could. Would have to cook way in de night or sometimes fore
day. Oose dey would take dey dinner rations wid dem to de
field. More or less, dey would cook it in de field. Yes'um,
dey would carry dey pots wid dem en cook right dere in de field
whe' dey was workin. Would boil pots en make bread, too. I
don' know how long dey had to work, mam, but I hear dem say dat
dey worked hard, cold or hot, rain or shine. Had to hoe cotton
en pick cotton en all such as dat. I don' know, mam, but de
white folks, I guess dey took it dat dey had plenty colored
people en dey Lord never meant for dem to do no work. You
know, white folks in dem days, dey made de colored people do."

Code No.
Project, 1885-(1)
Prepared by Annie Ruth Davis
Place, Marion, S.C.
Date, January 27, 1938

No. Words_____
Reduced from____words
Rewritten by
_____
Page 3.

100

"De people used to spin en weave, my Lord! Like today, it cloudy en rainy, dey couldn' work in de field en would have to spin dat day. Man, you would hear dat thing windin en I remember, I would stand dere en want to spin so bad, I never know what to do. Won' long fore I got to whe' I could use de shuttle en weave, too. I had a grandmother en when she would get to dat wheel, she sho know what she been doin. White folks used to give de colored people task to spin en I mean she could do dat spinnin. Yes'um, I here to tell you, dey would make de prettiest cloth in dat day en time. Old time people used to have a kind of dye dey called indigo en dey would color de cloth just as pretty as you ever did see."

"Den I recollects dat dey would have to shuck corn some of de days en wouldn' nobody work in de field dat day. Oh, my Lord, dey would have de big eats on dem days. Would have a big pot right out to de barn whe' dey was shuckin corn en would boil it full as it could hold wid such as peas en rice en collards. Would cook big bread, too, en would save a hog's head for dat purpose often times."

"Colored people didn' have no schools nowhe' in dat day en time. No'um, us didn' go to no church neither cause we was way off dere on de plantation en wasn' any church nowhe' bout dere, Miss. I likes to be truthful en I tellin you, when we was comin up, we never didn' know nothin 'cept what we catch from de old folks."

Code No.
Project, 1885-(1)
Prepared by Annie Ruth Davis
Place, Marion, S.C.
Date, January 27, 1938

No. Words_____
Reduced from___words
Rewritten by

101

Page 4.

"Old Massa, he used to come to de plantation drivin
his rockaway en my Lord a mercy, we chillun did love to run
en meet him. Dey used to have a great big gate to de lane
of de plantation en when we been hear him comin, we would go
a runnin en holler, 'Massa comin! Massa comin!' En he would
come ridin through de big gate en say, 'Yonder my little
niggers! How my little niggers? Come here en téll me how
you all.' Den we would go a runnin to him en try to tell him
what he ax us. Yes'um, we was sho pleased to see old Massa
cause we had to stay right dere on dat plantation all de time
round bout dat old woman what tended to us. Used to hear my
mother en my father speak bout dey had to get a ticket from
dey boss to go anywhe' dey wanted to go off de place. Pataroller
catch dem off de plantation somewhe' widout dat walkin ticket,
dey would whip dem most to death. Never didn' hear bout old
Massa whippin none of dem, but he was very tight on dem, my
father say. Cose he give dem abundance of rations en somethin
to eat all de time, but colored people sho been work for what
dey would get in dem days. Didn' get nothin dey never pay for.
It been like dis, what rations us parents would get, dat would
be to dey house en what we chillun been get would be to de old
woman's house what took care of us."

"Well, Miss, some people stays here wid me, but dey works
out en I tries to help dem out somehow. No,mam, we all stays
right here together en while dey on de job, I tries to look

Code No.
Project, 1885-(1)
Prepared by Annie Ruth Davis
Place, Marion, S.C.
Date, January 27, 1938

No. Words_____
Reduced from____words
Rewritten by
_____

102

Page 5.

out for de chillun. I just thinkin bout when we come to a
certain age, honey, it tough. Chillun is a heap of trouble,
I say. Well, I was de mother of five, but dey all dead 'cept
one. My husband, he been dead seven years. Yes'um, dis a bad
little girl settin here in my lap en dat one over dere in de
bed, he a boy what a right smart larger den dis one. (Little
girl just can stand alone).(Little boy wakes up). "Son, dere
you wantin to get up en I don' know whe' near a rag to put on
you is. Dere, you want a piece of bread fore you is dress.
Who undressed you last night nohow? Boy, you got to stand
dere en wait till your mamma come home cause I can' find none
your rags. What de matter wid you? You so hungry, you just
standin dere wid your mouth droolin dat way. Dere your bread
en tea on de bureau. Gwine on en get it." (Little boy's
breakfast consisted of a cold biscuit and a little cold coffee
poured in an empty coffee can. The little girl sat with a
clump of cold hominy in her hand on which she nibbled.)

    "Lord, I think what a blessin it would be if chillun dese
days was raise like dey used to be, Miss. Yes,mam, we had what
you call strict fathers en mothers den, but chillun ain' got
dem dese days. Oh, dey would whip you en put de lash to you
in dat day en time. Yes'um, Miss, if we never do right, my
father would put it to us. Sho meant what he say. Wouldn'
never whip you on Sunday though. Say dat he would get you
tomorrow. Den when Monday come, he would knock all bout like

Code No.
Project, 1885-(1)
Prepared by Annie Ruth Davis
Place, Marion, S.C.
Date, January 27, 1938

No. Words_____
Reduced from____words
Rewritten by
_____
Page 6.

103

he had forget, but toreckly he would call you up en he would sho work on you. Pa say, 'I'm not gwine let you catch me in no lie. When I tell you I gwine cut you, I gwine do it.' Miss, I is had my mother to hurt me so bad till I would just fall down en roll in de sand. Hurt! Dey hurt, dat dey did. Wouldn' whip you wid no clothes on neither. Would make you pull off. Yes, mam, I could sniffle a week, dey been cut me such licks. Thought dey had done me wrong, but dey know dey ain' been doin me wrong en I mean dey didn' play wid me."

"Miss, I think folks is livin too fast in de world today. Seems to me like all de young people is worser, I say. Well, I tell you, dey be ridin out all times of night en girls meetin up wid Miss Fortune. At least, our colored girls does. En don' care what dey do neither. Don' seem to care what dey do nor how dey do. De girls nowadays, dey gets dey livin. Girls settin higher den what dey makes demselves dese days."

Source: Josephine Bristow, colored, 73 years, Marion, S.C.

Personal interview by Annie Ruth Davis, Jan., 1938

ANNE BROOME

EX-SLAVE 87 YEARS OLD.

"Does you recollect de Galloway place just dis side of White Oak?
Well dere's where I was born. When? Can't name de 'zact year but my ma
say, no stork bird never fetch me but de fust railroad train dat come up
de railroad track, when they built de line, fetched me. She say I was a
baby, settin' on de cow-ketcher, and she see me and say to pa: 'Reubin,
run out dere and get our baby befo' her falls off and gets hurt under them
wheels! Do you know I believed dat tale 'til I was a big girl? Sure did,
'til white folks laugh me out of it!

"My ma was name Louisa. My marster was Billie Brice, but 'spect
God done write sumpin' else on he forehead by dis time. He was a cruel
marster; he whip me just for runnin' to de gate for to see de train run by.
My missus was a pretty woman, flaxen hair, blue eyes, name Mary Simonton,
'til she marry.

"Us live in a two-room plank house. Plenty to eat and enough to
wear 'cept de boys run 'round in their shirt tails and de girls just a
one-piece homespun slip on in de summer time. Dat was not a hardship then.
Us didn't know and didn't care nothin' 'bout a 'spectable 'pearance in
those days. Dats de truth, us didn't.

"Gran'pa name Obe; gran'ma, name Rachel. Shoes? A child never
have a shoe. Slaves wore wooden bottom shoes.

"My white folks went to New Hope Church. Deir chillun was mighty
good to us all. Dere was Miss Martha, her marry Doctor Madden, right here
at Winnsboro. Miss Mary marry Marster John Vinson, a little polite smilin'
man, nice man, though. Then Miss Jane marry Marster John Young. He passed

out, leavin' two lovely chillun, Kitty and Maggie. Both of them marry Caldwells. Dere was Marster Calvin, he marry Congfessman Wallace's daughter, Ellen. Then dere was Marster Jim and Marster William, de last went to Florida.

"It was a big place, I tell you, and heaps and heaps of slaves. Some times they git too many and sell them off. My old mistress cry 'bout dat but tears didn't count wid old marster, as long as de money come a runnin' in and de rations stayed in de smoke house.

"Us had a fine carriage. Sam was de driver. Us go to Concord one Sunday and New Hope de next. Had quality fair neighbors. Dere was de Cockerells, Piscopalians, dat 'tend St. John in Winnsboro, de Adgers, big buckra, went to Sion in Winnsboro. Marster Burr Cockerell was de sheriff. 'Members he had to hang a man once, right in de open jailyard. Then dere was a poor buckra family name Marshall. Our white folks was good to them, 'cause they say his pappy was close kin to de biggest Jedge of our country, John Marshall.

"When de slaves got bad off sick, marster send for Dr. Walter Brice, his kin folks. Some times he might send for Dr. Madden, him's son-in-law, as how he was.

"When de Yankees come, all de young marsters was off in de 'Federate side. I see them now, gallopin' to de house, canteen boxes on their hips and de bayonets rattlin' by deir sides. De fust thing they ask, was: 'You got any wine?' They search de house; make us sing: 'Good Old Time 'Ligion; put us to runnin' after de chickens and a cookin'. When they leave they burnt de gin house and everything in dere. They burn de smoke-house and wind up wid burnin' de big house.

"You through wid me now, boss? I sho' is glad of dat. Help all you kin to git me dat pension befo' I die and de Lord will bless you, honey. De Lord not gwine to hold His hand any longer 'ginst us. Us cleared de forests, built de railroads, cleaned up de swamps, and nursed de white folks. Now in our old ages, I hopes they lets de old slaves like me see de shine of some of dat money I hears so much talk 'bout. They say its free as de gift of grace from de hand of de Lord. Good mornin' and God bless you, will be my prayer always. Has you got a dime to give dis old nigger, boss?

MOM HAGAR

(Verbatim Conversation)

Mom Hagar Brown lives in her little weathered cabin on
forty odd acres left by her husband, Caleb Brown. Caleb died
in Georgia where he had been sent to the penitentiary for
stealing a hog that another man stole. Aunt Hagar has grands
settled all around her and she and the grands divide up the
acreage which is planted in corn, sweet potatoes, cotton, and
some highland rice. She ministers to them all when sick,
acts as mid-wife when necessary, and divides her all with her
kin and friends - white and black. She wages a war on
ground-moles, at which she laughs and says she resembles.
Ground-mole beans almost a foot long protect and decorate her
yard. She has apple and fig trees, and scuppernong grape
vines grow rank and try to climb all her trees.

(Monday morning she hobbles up on a stick - limping and
looking sick.) Comes in kitchen door.

Lillie: "Aunt Hagar, how you?"

Hagar: "Painful. Doctor tell me I got the tonsil. Want
to represent me one time and take them out. I
say, 'No Doctor! Get in hospital, can't get out!
Let me stay here till my change come.' Yeddy? I
ain't wuth! Ain't wuth! Ain't got a piece o'
sense. Yeddy? Ellen say she want God to take
she tomorrow? When you ready it's 'God take me

now!' All right son!" (Greeting Zackie who enters
kitchen.)

Zackie: "Aunt Hagar, how you feel?"

Hagar: "I ain't wuth son. How's all?"

Zackie: "Need a little more grits!"

Lillie: "Hear Zackie! Mom Hagar, that ain't hinder him
           ordering another!" (The fact that food is scarce
           doesn't limit Zackie's family.)

Hagar: "You hear bout this Jeremiah broke in somewhere -
           get all kinds likker and canned things and differ-
           ent thing?"

Zackie: "Must a broke in that place call 'Stumble Inn!'
           (Very seriously.) That Revenue man been there."

Hagar: "I yeddy last night! Say he there in news-paper.
           Mary say, ' see 'em in paper!' Mrs. White gone to
           child funeral. That been in paper too. Mary see
           that in paper. Easter say old lady gone dere.
           Doctor say better go. Child sick. Child seven
           years old. Fore they get there tell 'em say,
           'Child dead!'

           "People gone in patch to pick watermillon. Ain't
want child to go. You know chillun! Child gone in. Ain't
want 'em for go. You know. Child pick watermillon. Ketch
up one - I forgotten what pound they say. Roll. Roll duh

watermillion. Roll 'em on snake! They say, 'Snake bite 'em?'
Child say, 'No. Must a scratch.' See blood run on boy leg.
Child get unconscion that minute. Gone right out. Jess so.
Ease out so. I cry. I cry!"

Lillie: "You know 'em, Mom Hagar?"

Hagar: "No! No! Lill, fever got me! Cold get me till my
          rump dead. Got hospital boy rouse one time say,
          'Ma, less go home! Red stripe snake bite me.'"

Hagar: "Klu Klux?" (Chin cupped in hand - elbow on knee -
          looking way off -)

     "Reckon that the way them old timey people call 'em.
Have to run way, you go church. Going to come in to ketch
you or do any mischievous thing - come carry you place
they going beat you - in suit of white. Old white man to
Wilderness Plantation. Parish old man name. Treat his wife
bad. Come to house, ain't crack. Come right in suit of
white. Drag him out - right to Woodstock there where Mr.
Dan get shoot. Put a beating on that white man there till
he mess up! 'Oman never gone back to him yet!

     "A man wuz name (I forgot what the man name wuz) -
wuz a white man mess round wid a colored woman and they
didn't do a God thing but gone and put a beating on you,

darling! Come in. Grab you and go. Put a beating on you
till you can't see. Know they got a good grub to lick you
wid. They git done you can't sit down. Ain't going carry
you just for play with."

        "Mom Hagar, you wanter vote?"

Hagar: "Oh my God!"

        "Aunt Hagar are the colored people happier now
          than the old timey slavery time people?"

Hagar: "Young people now got the world by force. Don't
      care. Got more trick than law low. Tricky!
      Can't beat the old people. Can't equal to 'em.
      Some the young people you say 'AMEN' in church
      they make fun o' you. Every tub stand on his
      own bottom. Can't truss 'em.

        "Ma say some dem plan to run way. Say, 'Less
run! Less run!' Master ketch dem and fetch dem in. Lay
'em cross barrel. Beat dem till they wash in blood.
Fetch 'em back. Place 'em cross the barrel - hogsket
barrel - Christ! They ramp wash in blood! Beat Ma sister. He sister sickly. Never could clear task - like he
want. My Ma have to work he self to death to help Henritta
so sickly. Clear task to keep from beat. Some obersheer
mean. Oaks labor. (Meaning her Ma and ma's family were
laboring on Oaks Plantation - the plantation where Gov.

Joseph Allston and Theodosia his wife lived on Waccamaw)
Mother Sally Doctor. Ma got four chillun. One was Emmeline, one Getty, one Katrine one Hagar! I older than
Gob (Katrine). Could a call doctor for Gob if I had any
sense." (Big nuff to gone for doctor when Gob born.)

"Stay in the field!

Stay in the field!

Stay in the field till the war been end!"

(This is Aunt Hagar's favorite song)

Mom Hagar Brown - age 77

Murrells Inlet, S. C.

July 4th, 1937.

Project #-1655
Mrs. Genevieve W. Chandler
Murrells Inlet, S. C.
Georgetown County

390210

FOLKLORE   112

(Some recollections of Mom Hagar Brown)

Visitor: "Mom Hagar, how old did you say you were?"

Hagar: "Don't take care of my age! Had me gang of
chillun when ma die. I had Samuel, I had Elias, I had
Arthur, I had Beck. Oh, my God! Man, go way! I had
Sally! I had Sally again. I didn't want to give the
name 'Sally' again. Say, 'First Sally come carry girl.'
Ma say, 'Gin 'em name 'Sally!' I faid (afraid) that
other one come back for him. Had to do what Ma say.
Had to please 'em. Ma name Sally. Ma chillun Catrine,
Hagar, Emmeline, Gettie. I born Columbia. Come Freedom,
when we left Columbia, ma finer till we get in Charston.
Freedom come, battle till we get 'Oaks.' (Battled till
they reached the 'Oaks Plantation - -.') Stay there
till people gin (begin) move bout. Come Watsaw. Gone
'Collins Creek.' In the 'Reb Time' you know, when they
sell you bout - Massa sell you all about. Broke
through them briar and branch and thing to go to church.
Them patrol get you. Church 'Old Bethel.' You don't
know 'em. Been gone!

    "I yeddy ma! (heard my mother) Ma say, 'I too
glad my chillun aint been here Rebs time! Gin you task
you rather drown than not done that task! Ma say Auntie
poor we weak creeter, couldn't strain. Ma had to strain
to fetch sister up with her task. Dere (there) in rice-

field. Ma say they on flat going to islant (island), see
cloud, pray God send rain! When rooster crow, say they
pray God to stop 'em! Rooster crow, broke up wedder!
When rooster crow, scare 'em. Broke up rain! Ma say
they drag the pot in the river when the flat going cross.
Do this to make it rain. Massa! Don't done you task,
driver wave that whip, put you over the barrel, beat you
so blood run down! I wouldn't take 'em! Ma say, 'I too
glad my chillun aint born then!'

"Any cash money? Where you gwine get 'em? Only cash
the gospel! Have to get the gospel. Give you cloth!
Give you ration! Jess (just according) many chillun you
got. Ma say chillun feed all the corn to the fowl.
Chillun say, 'Papa love he fowl!

            Papa love he fowl!
            Three peck a day!
            Three peck a day!

"Parent come to door. Not a grain of corn leave!
Poor people! Come, drop! Not a grain! Everybody on
the hill help. One give this; one give that. Handle 'em
light! (Very careful with victuals). Gone you till
Saddy (Saturday.) (Will last you until Saturday when
you are rationed again.)

"When Ma get down, she say, 'I gone leave! I gone

leave here now! But, oh, Hagar! Be a mudder and fadder
for Katrine!'

"I say, (I call Katrine 'Gob') I say, 'Better tell
Gob to look atter me!'

"Ma say, 'When I gone I ax the Master when he take me,
to send drop o' rain to let true believer know I gone to
Glory!'

"When they lift the body to take 'em to the church,
rain, 'Tit! Tit! Tit! Tit!' on the house! At the gate,
moon shine out! Going to the church! Bury to the 'Oaks.'

"Gob say, 'Titty, all you chillun bury at Oaks. Ma to
Oaks. How come you wanter bury Watsaw?"

"I say, 'When the trumpet sound, I yeddy!' (When the
trumpet sounds, I'll hear it!)

"I marry right to Collins Creek hill. Big dance out
the door! I free! I kick up! Ma, old rebs time people!"

> Mom Hagar Brown
> Age - (She says 'Born first o'
> Freedom' but got her age from
> a contemporary and reported 77)
> Murrells Inlet, S. C.

EX-SLAVE STORY

(Verbatim)

"My old man can 'member things and tell you things and he word carry. We marry to Turkey Hill Plantation. Hot supper. Cake, wine, and all. Kill cow, hog, chicken and all. That time when you marry, so much to eat! Finance wedding! Now -

"We 'lamp-oil chillun'; they 'lectric light' chillun now! We call our wedding 'lamp-oil wedding'. Hall jam full o' people; out-of-door jam full. Stand before the chimbley.

"When that first war come through, we born. I don't know just when I smell for come in the world.

"Big storm? Yinnah talk big storm hang people up on tree? (Noah!) Shake? I here in house. House gone, 'Rack-a-rack-a-racker!'

"My husband run out - with me and my baby left in bed! Baby just come in time of the shake.

"When I first have sense, I 'member I walk on the frost bare-feet. Cow-belly shoe.

"My husband mother have baby on the flat going to Marion and he Auntie Cinda have a baby on that flat.

"From yout (youth) I been a Brown and marry a Brown; title never change.

"Old timey sing?

1.   "Wish I had a hundred dog
        And half wuz hound!
        Take it in my fadder field

And we run the rabbit down!

Chorus: Now he hatch

He hatch!

He hatch!

And I run the rabbit down!

2.   I wish I had a hundred head o' dog

And half of them wuz hound

I'd take 'em back in my bacco field

And run the rabbit down.

Chorus: Now he hatch - he hatch!

He hatch - he hatch!

Now he hatch - he hatch!

And I run them rabbit down!"

That wuz a sing we used to have on the plantation. Then
we make up sing - we have sing fer chillun. Make 'em go
sleep. Every one have his own sing.

"Bye-o-baby!

Go sleepy!

Bye-o-baby!

Go sleepy!

What a big alligator

Coming to catch

This one boy!"

Diss here the Watson one boy child!

Bye-e-baby go sleepy!

What a big alligator

Coming to catch this one boy!

Emmie Jordan: "Missus, I too plague with bad heart trouble
to give you the sing!"

Song and conversation Given by

Mom Louisa Brown (Born time of 'Reb
                    people War')
Waverly Mills, S. C.

Near - Parkersville, S. C.

Project #-1655
Jessie A. Butler
Charleston, S. C.

Approximately 930 words ·

FOLKLORE

Stories from Ex-slaves
Henry Brown
Ex-slave Age 79

Henry Brown, negro caretaker of the Gibbes House, at the foot of Grove
street, once a part of Rose Farm, is a splendid example of a type once fre-
quently met with in the South. Of a rich brown complexion, aquiline of fea-
ture, there is none of the "Gullah" about Henry. He is courteous and kindly
in his manner, and speaks more correctly than the average negro.

"My father was Abram Brown, and my mother's name was Lucy Brown," he said,
"They were slaves of Dr. Arthur Gordon Rose. My grandfather and grandmother
were grown when they came from Africa, and were man and wife in Africa. I
was born just about two years before the war so I don't remember anything about
slavery days, and very little about war times, except that we were taken to
Deer Pond, about half mile from Columbia. Dr. Rose leased the place from Dr.
Ray, and took his family there for safety. My mother died while he was at
Deer Pond, and was buried there, but all the rest of my people is buried right
here at Rose Farm. My two brothers were a lot older than me, and were in the
war. After the war my brother Tom was on the police force, he was a sergeant,
and they called him Black Sergeant. My brother Middleton drove the police wagon:
they used to call it Black Maria.

"My father, Abram Brown, was the driver or head man at Rose plantation.
Dr. Rose thought a heap of him, and during the war he put some of his fine
furniture and other things he brought from England in my father's house and
told him if the Yankees came to say the things belonged to him. Soon after

that the soldiers came. They asked my father who the things belonged to

and he said they belonged to him. The soldiers asked him who gave them to

him, and he said his master gave them to him. The Yankees told him that they

thought he was lying, and if he didn't tell the truth they would kill him, but

he wouldn't say anything else so they left him alone and went away.

"Work used to start on the plantation at four o'clock in the morning,

when the people went in the garden. At eight or nine o'clock they went into

the big fields. Everybody was given a task of work. When you finished your

task you could quit. If you didn't do your work right you got a whipping.

"The babies were taken to the negro house and the old women and young

colored girls who were big enough to lift them took care of them. At one

o'clock the babies were taken to the field to be nursed, then they were brought

back to the negro house until the mothers finished their work, then they

would come for them.

"Dr. Rose gave me to his son, Dr. Arthur Barnwell Rose, for a Christmas

present. After the war Dr. Rose went back to England. He said he couldn't

stay in a country with so many free negroes. Then his son Dr. Arthur Barnwell

Rose had the plantation. Those was good white people, good white people.

" The colored people were given their rations once a week, on Monday, they

got corn, and a quart of molasses, and three pounds of bacon, and sometimes

meat and peas. They had all the vegetables they wanted; they grew them in

the gardens. When the boats first came in from Africa with the slaves, a

big pot of peas was cooked and the people ate it with their hands right from

the pot.   The slaves on the plantation went to meeting two nights a week and
on Sunday they went to Church, where they had a white preacher Dr. Rose hired
to preach to them.

After the war when we came back to Charleston I went to work as a chimney-
sweep. I was seven years old then. They paid me ten cents a story. If a house
had two stories I got twenty cents; if it had three stories I got thirty cents.
When I got too big to go up the chimneys I went back to Rose plantation. My
father was still overseer or driver. I drove a cart and plowed. Afterwards I
worked in the phosphate mines, then came back here to take care of the garden
and be caretaker. I planted all these Cherokee roses you see round here, and
I had a big lawn of Charleston grass. I aint able to keep it like I used to."

Henry is intensely religious. He says "the people don't notice God now
because they're free." "Some people say there aint no hell," he continued,
"but I think there must be some kind of place like that, because you got to go
some place when you leave this earth, and you got to go to the master that you
served when you were here. If you serve God and obey His commandments then
you go to Him, but if you don't pay any attention to what he tells you in His
Book, just do as you choose and serve the devil, then you got to go to him.
And it don't make any difference if you're poor or rich, it don't matter what
the milliner (millionaire) man says."

He seemed so proud of his garden, with its broad view across the Ashley
River, showing his black walnut, pear and persimmon trees, grape vines and roses,
that the writer said, "Henry, you know a poet has said that we are nearer God

in the garden than anywhere else on earth." "Well ma'am, you see," he

replied, with a winning smile, "that's where God put us in the first place."

S-260-264-N
Project #1655
Augustus Ladson
Charleston,S.C.

EX-SLAVE BORN 1857

GRAND PARENTS CAME DIRECTLY FROM AFRICA

I was nickname' durin' the days of slavery.My name was Henry but they call' me Toby.My sister,Josephine,too was nickname' an' call' Jessee.Our mistress had a cousin by that name.My oldes' bredder was a Sergeant on the Charleston Police Force around 1868.I had two other sister',Louise an' Rebecce.

My firs' owner was Arthur Barnwell Rose.Then Colonel A.G.Rhodes bought the plantation who sol' it to Capen Frederick W.Wagener.James Sottile then got in possession who sol' it to the DeCostas.an' a few weeks ago Mrs.Albert Gallitin Simms,who I'm tol' is a former member of Congress,bought it.Now I'm wonderin' if she is goin' to le' me stay.I hope so 'cus I'm ol' now en can't work.

My pa was name' Abraham Brown;he was bo'n on Coals Islan' in Beaufort County.Colonel Rhodes bought him for his driver,then he move here.I didn't know much 'bout him;he didn't live so long afta slavery 'cus he was ol.

Colonel Rhodes had a son an' a daughter.The son went back to England afta his death an' the daughter went to Germany with her husban'.They ain't never come back so the place was sol' for tax.

Durin' the war we was carry to Deer Pond,twelve miles on dis side of Columbia.W'en the war was end' pa brought my sister,Louise,Rebecca,who was too small to work,Josephine an' me ,home.All my people is long-lifted .My grand pa an' grand ma on pa side come right from Africa.They was stolen an' brought here. They use to tell us of how white men had pretty cloth on boats which they was to exchange for some of their o'nament'.W'en they take the o'nament' to the boat they was carry way down to the bottom an' was lock' in. They was anchored on or

EX-SLAVE cont'd.

near Sullivan's Islan' w'ere they been feed like dogs. A big pot was use' for cookin'.In that pot peas was cook' an' lef' to cool.Everybody went to the pot with the han's an' all eat frum the pot.

I was bo'n two years before the war an' was seven w'en it end.That was in 1857.I never went to school but five months in my life,but could learn easy.Very seldom I had to be tel' to do the same thing twice.

The slaves had a plenty o' vegetables all the time.Master planted t'ree acres jus' for the slaves which was attended to in the mornin's before tas' time.All provision was made as to the distribution on Monday evenin's afta tas'.

My master had two place:one on Big Islan' an' on Coals Islan' in Beaufort County.He didn't have any overseer.My pa was his driver.

Pa say this place was given to Mr.Rhodes with a thousand acres of lan' by England.But it dwindled to thirty-five w'en the other was taken back by England.

There wasn't but ten slaves on this plantation.The driver call' the slaves at four so they could git their breakfas' .They always work the garden firs' an' at seven go in the co'n an' cotton fiel'.Some finish their tas' by twelve an' others work' 'til seven but had the tas' to finish.No one was whip' 'less he needed it;no one else could whip master' slaves .He wouldn't stan' for it.We had it better then than now 'cause white men lynch an' burn now an' do other things they couldn't do then.They shoot you down like dogs now,an' nothin' said or done.

No slave was suppose' to be whip' in Charleston except at the Sugar House.There was a jail for whites ,but if a slave ran away an' got there he could disown his master an' the State wouldn't le' him take you.

EX-SLAVE cont'd.

All collud people had to have a pass w'en they went travelin';free as well as slaves.If one didn't the patrollers ,who was hired by rich white men would give you a good whippin' an' sen' you back home.My pa didn't need any one to write his pass 'cause he could write as well as master.How he got his education,I didn't know.

Sat'day was a workin' day but the tas' was much shorter than other days.men didn't have time to frolic 'cause they had to rin' roed for the rambly;master never give 'nough to las' the whole week.A peck o' co'n,t'ree pound o' beacon,quart o' molasses,a quart o' salt,an' a pack o' tobacco was given the men.The wife got the same thing but chillun accordin' to age.Only one holiday slaves had an' that was Christmas.

Co'nshuckin' parties was conducted by a group of fa'mers who take their slaves or sen' them to the neighborin' ones 'til all the co'n was shuck'. Each one would furnish food 'nough for all slaves at his party.Some use to have nothin' but bake potatas an' some kind of vegetable.

An unmarried young man was call' a half-han'.W'en he want to marry he jus' went to master an' say there's a gal he would like to have for wife. Master would say yes an' that night more chicken would be fry an' everything eatable would be prepare' at master' expense.The couple went home afta the supper,without any readin' of matrimony,man an' wife.

A man once married his ma an' didn't know it.He was sell from her w'en 'bout eight years old.when he grow to a young man ,slavery then was over,he met this woman who he like' an' so they were married.They was mar ried a month w'en one night they started to tell of their experiences an'

EX-SLAVE cont'd.

how many times they was sol'.The husban' tol' how he was sol' from his mother
who liked him dearly.He tol' how his ma faint' w'en they took him away an' how
his master then use to bran' his baby slaves at a year ol'.W'en he showed her
the bran' she faint' 'cause she then realize'that she had married her son.

Slaves didn't have to use their own remedy for sickness for good doctors been hired to look at them.There was,as is,though,some weed use for fever
an' headache as:blacksnake root,turrywork,jimpsin weed,one that tie' on the
head which bring sweat from you like hail,an' hickory leaf.If the hickory is
keep on the head too long it will blister it.

W'en the war was fightin' the white men burn the bridge at the foot
of Spring Street so the Yankees couldn't git over but they buil' pontoos while
some make the horses swim 'cross.One night while at Deer Pond,I hear something
like thunder until 'bout eleven the next day.W'en the thing I t'ought was
thunder stop',master tell us that evenin' we was free.I wasn't surprise to
know for as little as I was I know the Yankees was goin' to free us with the
help of God.

I was married twice,an' had two gals an' a boy with firs' wife.I have
t'ree boys with the second;the younges' is jus' eight.

Lincoln did jus' what God inten' him to do,but I think nothin' 'bout
Calhoun on 'account of what he say in one of his speech 'bout collud people.
He said:"keep the niggers down."

To see collud boys goin' 'round now with paper an' pencil in their
han's don't look real to me.Durin' slavery he would be whip' 'til not a skin
was lef' on his body.

My pa was a preacher why I become a christian so early;he preach' on
the plantation to the slaves.On Sunday the slaves went to the white church.
He use to tell us of hell an' how hot it is.I was so 'fraid of hell 'til I

EX-SLAVE cont'd.

was always tryin' to do the right thing so I couldn't go to that terrible place.

I don't care 'bout this worl' an' its vanities 'cause the Great Day is comin' w'en I shall lay down an' my stammerin' tongue goin' to lie silent in my head.I want a house not made with han's but eternal in the Heavens.That Man up there,is all I need;I'm goin' to still trus' Him.Before the comin' of Chris' men was kill' for His name sake;today they curse Him.It's nearly time for the world to come to en' for He said "bout two thousand years I shall come again" an' that time is fas' approacnin'.

SOURCE

Interview with Henry Brown,637 Grove Street.He is much concerned with the Scottsboro Case and discusses the invasion of Italy into defenseless Ethiopia intelligently.

JOHN C. BROWN AND ADELINE BROWN
EX-SLAVES 86 YEARS AND 96 YEARS OLD.

John C. Brown and his wife, Adeline, who is eleven years older than
himself, live in a ramshackle four-room frame house in the midst of a cotton
field, six miles west of Woodward, S. C. John assisted in laying the founda-
tion and building the house forty-four years ago. A single china-berry tree,
gnarled but stately, adds to, rather than detracts from, the loneliness of
the dilapidated house. The premises and thereabout are owned by the Federal
Land Bank. The occupants pay no rent. Neither of them are able to work.
They have been fed by charity and the W.P.A. for the past eighteen months.

(John talking)

" Where and when I born? Well, dat'll take some 'hear say', Mister.
I never knowed my mammy. They say she was a white lady dat visited my old
marster and mistress. Dat I was found in a basket, dressed in nice baby
clothes, on de railroad track at Dawkins, S. C. De engineer stop de train,
got out, and found me sumpin' like de princess found Moses, but not in de
bulrushes. Him turn me over to de conductor. De conductor carry me to de
station at Dawkins, where Marse Tom Dawkins come to meet de train dat mornin'
and claim me as found on his land. Him say him had de best right to me. De
conductor didn't 'ject to dat. Marse Tom carry me home and give me to Miss
Betsy. Dat was his wife and my mistress. Her always say dat Sheton Brown
was my father. He was one of de slaves on de place; de carriage driver.
After freedom he tell me he was my real pappy. Him took de name of Brown

and dat's what I go by.

" My father was a ginger-bread colored man, not a full-blooded nigger. Dat's how I is altogether yellow. See dat lady over dere in dat chair? Dat's my wife. Her brighter skinned than I is. How come dat? Her daddy was a full-blooded Irishman. He come over here from Ireland and was overseer for Marse Bob Clowney. He took a fancy for Adeline's mammy, a bright 'latto gal slave on de place. White women in them days looked down on overseers as poor white trash. Him couldn't git a white wife but made de best of it by puttin' in his spare time a honeyin' 'round Adeline's mammy. Marse Bob stuck to him, and never 'jected to it.

" When de war come on, Marse Richard, de overseer, shoulder his gun as a soldier and, as him was educated more than most of de white folks, him rise to be captain in de Confederate Army. It's a pity him got kilt in dat war.

" My marster, Tom Dawkins, have a fine mansion. He owned all de land 'round Dawkins and had 'bout 200 slaves, dat lived in good houses and was we well fed. My pappy was de man dat run de mill and grind de wheat and corn into flour and meal. Him never work in de field. He was 'bove dat. Him 'tend to de ginnin' of de cotton and drive de carriage.

" De Yankees come and burn de mansion, de gin-house and de mill. They take all de sheep, mules, cows, hogs and even de chickens. Set de slaves free and us niggers have a hard time ever since.

" My black stepmammy was so mean to me dat I run away. I didn't know where to go but landed up, one night, at Adeline's mammy's and steppappy's house, on Marse Bob Clowney's place. They had been slaves of Marse Bob and was livin' and workin' for him. I knock on de door. Mammy Charity, dat's

Adeline's mammy, say: 'Who dat?' I say: 'Me'. Her say: 'Who is me?' I say: 'John'. Her say: 'John who?' I say: 'Just John'. Her say: 'Adeline, open de door, dat's just some poor boy dat's cold and hungry. Charity is my fust name. Your pappy ain't come yet but I'll let dat boy in 'til he come and see what he can do 'bout it.'

"When Adeline open dat door, I look her in de eyes. Her eyes melt towards me wid a look I never see befo' nor since. Mind you, I was just a boy fourteen, I 'spects, and her a woman twenty-five then. Her say: 'You darlin' little fellow; come right in to de fire.' Oh, my! She took on over me! Us wait 'til her pappy come in. Then him say: 'What us gonna do wid him?' Adeline say: 'Us gonna keep him.' Pappy say: 'Where he gonna sleep?' Adeline look funny. Mammy say: 'Us'll fix him a pallet by de fire.' Adeline clap her hands and say: 'You don't mind dat, does you boy?' I say: 'No ma'am, I is slept dat way many a time.'

"Well, I work for Marse Bob Clowney and stayed wid Adeline's folks two years. I sure made myself useful in dat family. Never 'spicioned what Adeline had in her head, 'til one day I climbed up a hickory nut tree, flail de nuts down, come down and was helpin' to pick them up when she bump her head 'ginst mine and say: 'Oh, Lordy!' Then I pat and rub her head and it come over me what was in dat head! Us went to de house and her told de folks dat us gwine to marry.

"Her led me to de altar dat nex' Sunday. Gived her name to de preacher as Adeline Cabean. I give de name of John Clowney Brown. Marse Bob was dere and laugh when de preacher call my name, 'John Clowney Brown'.

"Our chillun come pretty fast. I was workin' for $45.00 a year, wid rations. Us had three pounds of bacon, a peck of meal, two cups of flour, one quart of 'lasses, and one cup of salt, a week.

"Us never left Marse Robert as long as him lived. When us have four chillun, him increase de amount of flour to four cups and de 'lasses to two quarts. Then him built dis house for de old folks and Adeline and de chillun to live in. I help to build it forty-four years ago. Our chillun was Clarice, Jim, John, Charity, Tom, Richard, and Adeline.

"I followed Marse Robert Clowney in politics, wore a red shirt, and voted for him to go to de Legislature. Him was 'lected dat time but never cared for it no more.

"Adeline b'long to de church. Always after me to jine but I can't believe dere is anything to it, though I believes in de law and de Ten Commandments. Preacher calls me a infidel. Can't help it. They is maybe got me figured out wrong. I believes in a Great Spirit but, in my time, I is seen so many good dogs and hosses and so many mean niggers and white folks, dat I 'clare, I is confused on de subject. Then I can't believe in a hell and everlastin' brimstone. I just think dat people is lak grains of corn; dere is some good grains and some rotten grains. De good grains is res'rected, de rotten grains never sprout again. Good people come up again and flourish in de green fields of Eden. Bad people no come up. Deir bodies and bones just make phosphate guano, 'round de roots of de ever bloomin' tree of life. They lie so much in dis world, maybe de Lord will just make 'lie' soap out of them. What you think else they would be fit for?"

INTERVIEW WITH EX-SLAVE
Age 88 - 90

_____

Mary Frances Brown is a typical product of the old school of trained
house servants, an unusual delicate type, somewhat of the Indian cast, to
which race she is related. She is always clean and neat, a refined old
soul, as individuals of that class often are. Her memory, sight and hearing
are good for her advanced age.

"Our home Marlboro. Mas Luke Turnage was my master - Marlboro-Factory-
Plantation name 'Beauty Spot'. My missis was right particular about neat and
clean. She raise me for a house girl. My missis was good to me, teach me
ebbery ting, and take the Bible and learn me Christianified manners, charity,
and behaviour and good respect, and it with me still.

"We didn't have any hard times, our owners were good to us - no over share
(overseer) and no whippin' - he couldn't stan' that. I live there 'til two
year after freedom; how I come to leave, my mother sister been sick, and she
ask mother to send one of us, an she send me. My mother been Miss Nancy cook.
Miss Nancy was Mas Luke's mother - it take me two years learning to eat the
grub they cook down here in Charleston. I had to learn to eat these little
piece of meat - we had a dish full of meat; the big smoke house was lined from
the top down. (Describing how the meat hung) I nebber accustom to dese little
piece of meat, so - what dey got here. Missis, if you know smoke house, didn't
you find it hard? My master had 'til he didnIt know what to do with. My white
people were Gentile." (Her tone implied that she considered them the acme of
gentle folks).   "I don't know what the other people were name that didn't have

as much as we had - but I know my people were Gentile!"

Just here her daughter and son appeared, very unlike their mother in type. The daughter is quite as old looking as her mother; the son, a rough stevedore. When the writer suggested that the son must be a comfort, she looked down sadly and said in a low tone, as if soliloquizing, "He way is he way." Going back to her former thought, she said, "All our people were good. Mas Luke was the worse one." (This she said with an indulgent smile) "Cause he was all the time at the Race ground or the Fair ground.

"Religion rules Heaven and Earth, an there is no religion now - harricanes an washin-aways is all about. Ebberything is change. Dis new name what they call grip is pleurisy-cold - putrid sore-throat is called somethin' - yes, diptheria. Cuttin (surgery) come out in 1911! They kill an they cure, an they save an they loss.

"My Gran'ma trained with Indians - she bin a Indian, an Daniel C. McCall bought her. She nebber loss a baby." (the first Indian relationship that the writer can prove) "You know Dr. Jennings? Ebberybody mus' know him. After he examine de chile an de mother, an 'ee alright, he hold de nurse responsible for any affection (infection) that took place.

"Oh! I know de spiritual - but Missis, my voice too weak to sing - dey aint in books; if I hear de name I can sing - 'The Promise Land', Oh, how Mas Joel Easterling (born 1796) use to love to sing dat!

Project #1655
Martha S. Pinckney
Charleston, S. C.

FOLKLORE

Page   3

133

"I am bound for de Promise Land!

Oh! who will arise an go with me?

I am bound for the Promise Land!

I've got a mother in the Promise Land,

My mother calls me an I mus go,

To meet her in the Promise Land!"

SOURCE: Mary Frances Brown, Age 88-90,   East Bay Street, Charleston,
         S. C.

Project #-1655
Cassels R. Tiedeman
Charleston, S. C.

INTERVIEW WITH AN EX*SLAVE

Mary Frances Brown, about ninety years of age, born in
slavery, on the plantation of Luke Turnage, in Marlboro
County, was raised as a house-servant and shows today evi-
dence of most careful training. Her bearing is rather a
gentle refindd type, seemingly untouched by the squalor
in which she lives. She willingly gives freely of her
small store of strength to those around her.

Her happiest days seem to have been those of her early
youth, for when she was questioned about the present times,
and even about those closely associated with her today she
bowed her head and said: "Deir way is deir way. O! let me
tell you now, de world is in a haad (hard) time, wust
(worse) den it eber (ever) been, but religion! It ebery-
where in Hebben an' in de ert (earth) too, if you want em.
De trouble is you ain't want em; 'e right dere jes de same
but de time done pass when dis generation hold wid anyt'ing
but de debbul. When I a gal, grown up, I had a tight
missus dat raise me, you hab to keep clean round her, she
good an' kind an' I lub her yet, but don't you forgit to
mind what she say.

"My massa, he 'low no whipping on de plantation, he talk
heap an' he scold plenty, but den he hab to. Dere was haad
time for two year after de war was ober (over) but after
dat it better den it is now. Dis is de wust time eber. I
ain't eber git use to de wittle (victual) you hab down here.

I lib ober Mount Pleasant twenty five year after I come from de old place up Marlboro, den I come to Charleston.

"Dey were happy time back dere. My massa, he run round ebery way, spend plenty money on horse race, he gib good time to eberybody an' tell us we mus' tek good care of de missus when he ain't dere. An de wittles we hab I ain't nebber see de lak no time. Dem were de times to lib. I old now but I ain't forgit what my missus larn (learn) me. It right here in me."

Mary Frances was asked if she could sing spirituals. The following is one that she sang in a very high pitched wavering voice and then she complained of shortness of breath on account of her heart.

"We got a home ober dere,

Come an' let us go,

Come an' let us go,

Where pleasure neber (never) die.

Chorus: "Oh! let us go where pleasure neber die,

Neber die,

Come and let us go,

Where pleasure neber die, neber die.

"Mother is gone ober dere,

Mother is gone ober dere,

Where pleasure neber die,

Where pleasure neber die.

Chorus;

"Father is gone ober dere,

Father is gone ober dere,

Where pleasure neber die,

Where pleasure neber die,

Chorus:

"Sister is gone ober dere,

Sister is gone ober dere,

Where pleasure neber die,

Where pleasure neber die,

Chorus:

"Brudder is gone ober dere,

Brudder is gone ober dere,

Where pleasure neber die,

Where pleasure neber die,

Chorus:

Source: Interview with Mary Frances Brown, 83 East Bay St.,

Charleston, S. C.   (age - 90)

Code No.
Project, 1885-(1)
Prepared by Annie Ruth Davis
Place, Marion, S.C.
Date, July 8, 1937

No. ~~Words~~
Reduced from____words
Rewritten by

MOM SARA BROWN
Ex-Slave, 85 years   390174

"Oh, my God, de doctors have me in slavery time. Been
here de startin of de first war. I belong to de Cusaac dat
live 15 miles low Florence on de road what take you on to
Georgetown. I recollects de Yankees come dere in de month
of June en free de colored peoples."

"My white folks give me to de doctors in dem days to
try en learn me for a nurse. Don' know exactly how old I
was in dat day en time, but I can tell you what I done. My
Lord, child, can' tell dat. Couldn' never tell how many
baby I bring in dis world, dey come so fast. I betcha I
got more den dat big square down dere to de courthouse full
of em. I nurse 13 head of chillun in one family right here
in dis town. You see dat all I ever did have to do. Was
learnt to do dat. De doctor tell me, say, when you call to
a 'oman, don' you never hesitate to go en help her en you
save dat baby en dat mother both. Dat what I is always try
to do. Heap of de time just go en let em pay me by de chance.
Oh, my Lord, a 'oman birth one of dem babies here bout two
weeks ago wid one of dem veil over it face. De Lord know
what make dat, I don', but dem kind of baby sho wiser den de
other kind of baby. Dat thing look just like a thin skin dat
stretch over de baby face en come down low it's chin. Have
to take en pull it back over it's forehead en den de baby can
see en holler all it ever want to. My blessed, honey, wish

Code No.
Project, 1885-(1)
Prepared by Annie Ruth Davis
Place, Marion, S.C.
Date, July 8, 1937

No. Words _____
Reduced from ___ words
Rewritten by
_____
Page 2.

138

I had many a dollar as I see veil over baby face. Sho know
all bout dem kind of things."

"Oh, honey, I tell you de people bless dis day en time.
Don' know nothin bout how to be thankful enough for what dey
have dese days. I tell de truth de peoples sho had to scratch
bout en make what dey had in slavery time. Baby, dey plant
patches of okra en parch dat en make what coffee dey have. Den
dey couldn' get no shoes like dey hab dese days neither. Just
make em out of de hide of dey own cows dat dey butcher right
dere on de plantation. Coase de peoples had plenty sometin to
eat like meat en turkey en chicken en thing like dat. Oh, my
God, couldn' see de top of de smoke house for all de heap of
meat dey have in dem times. En milk en butter, honey, dey
didn' never be widout plenty of dat. De peoples bout here
dese days axes ten cents a quart for sweet milk en five cents
a quart for old sour clabber. What you think bout dat? Dat
how-come people have to hunt jobs so mucha dese days. Have
to do some sorta work cause you know dey got to put sometin
in dey mouth somewhe' or another. Oh, my child, slavery days
was troublesome times. Sugar en salt never run free wid de
peoples den neither. I know de day been here when salt was
so scarce dat dey had to go to de seashore en get what salt
dey had. I gwine to tell you all bout dat. Dey hitch up two
horses to a wagon en den dey make another horse go in front of

Code No.
Project, 1885-(1)
Prepared by Annie Ruth Davis
Place, Marion, S.C.
Date, July 8, 1937

No. Words_____
Reduced from___words
Rewritten by_____

139

Page 3.

de wagon to rest de other horses long de way. Dey mostly
go bout on a Monday en stay three days. Boil dat salty
water down dere en fetch two en three of dem barrel of salt
back wid em dey get dat way. It was just like dis, it take
heap of salt when dey had dem big hog-killin days. En de
sugar, dey make dat too. Made de sugar in lil blocks dat
dey freeze just like dey freeze ice dis day en_time. I
know dey do dat - know it. Dey make molasses en some of
it would be lighter den de other en dey freeze dat en make
de prettiest lil squares just like de ice you see dese days.
Dey have sometin to freeze it in. Dis here old black mammy
know heap of things you ain' never hear bout. Oh, baby, de
peoples sho bless dese days."

"Oh, my God, de colored peoples worship to de white folks
church in slavery time. You know dat Hopewell Church over de
river dere, dat a slavery church. Dat whe' I go to church den
wid my white folks. I had a lil chair wid a cowhide bottom
dat I always take everywhe' I go wid me. If I went to church,
dat chair go in de carriage wid me en den I take it in de
church en set right by de side of my Miss. Dat how it was in
slavery time. Oh, my Lord, dere a big slavery people graveyard dere to dat Hopewell Church."

"Honey, you mind if I smoke my pipe a lil whilst I settin
here talkin wid you. I worry so much wid dis high blood dese

Code No.
Project, 1885-(1)
Prepared by Annie Ruth Davis
Place, Marion, S.C.
Date, July 8, 1937

No. Words
Reduced from   words
Rewritten by

Page 4.

140

days en a ringin in my ears dat my pipe de only thing dat does seem to satisfy my soul. I tell you dat high blood a bad thing. It get such a hold on me awhile back dat I couldn' do nothin, couldn' pick cotton, couldn' say my - me, couldn' even say, God a mighty - thing pretty. Oh, I don' know. I start smokin pipe long time ago when I first start nursin babies. Had to do sometin like dat den."

"No, Lord, I never believe nothin bout dat but what God put here. I hear some people say dey was conjure, but I don' pay no attention to dey talk. Dey say somebody poison em for sometin dey do, but dere ain' nobody do dat. God gwine to put you down when he get ready. Ain' nobody else do dat."

"Oh, my Lord, I been here a time. I sho been here a time en I thank de Lord I here dis day en time. I can thread my needle good as ever I could en I ain' have no speck neither. Sew night en day. De chillun have dey lamp dere studyin en I hab my lamp dere sewin. My old Miss learnt me to sew when I stay right in de house wid her all de time. I stay bout white folks all my life en dat how-come I so satisfy when I wid em."

Source: Mom Sara Brown, age 85, ex-slave, Marion, S.C.
        Personal interview, June 1937.

Code No.
Project, 1885-(1)
Prepared by Annie Ruth Davis
Place, Marion, S.C.
Date, September 10, 1937

No. Words
Reduced from___words
Rewritten by

141

Page 1.

MOM SARA BROWN
Ex-Slave, 85 Years

390281

"I stay in house over dere cross Catfish Swamp on
Miss Addie McIntyre place. Lives wid dis granddaughter
dat been sick in bed for four weeks, but she mendin some
now. She been mighty low, child. It start right in here
(chest) en run down twixt her shoulder. She had a tear up
cold too, but Dr. Dibble treat her en de cough better now.
She got three chillun dere dat come just like steps. One
bout like dat en another like dat en de other bout like dis."

"De house we stay in a two room house wid one of dese
end chimney. All sleep in de same room en cook en eat in de
other room. My bed on one side en Sue bed on de other side.
Put chillun on quilts down on de floor in de other end of de
room. Baby, whe' dem curtains you say you gwine give me? I
gwine hang dese up in Sue room. Dey help me fix up de room
nice en decent like."

"It all on me to feed en clothe both dem chillun en de
baby too. It just too much on me old as I is. Can' do nothin
worth to speak bout hardly dese days. Can' hold my head down
cause dis high blood worries me so much. It get too hot, can'
iron. If ain' too hot, I makes out to press my things somehow
en sweep my yard bout. Sometimes I helps little bit wid doctor
case, but not often. Can wash de baby en de mother, but can'

Code No.   No. Words_____
Project, 1885-(1)   Reduced from___words
Prepared by Annie Ruth Davis   Rewritten by
Place, Marion, S.C.   142
Date, September 10, 1937   Page 2.

do no stayin up at night. No, baby, can' do no settin up
at night."

"I tries to catch all what little I can to help along
cause dat how I was raise up. Government truck brings me
little somethin once a month pack up in packages like dry
milk en oatmeal en potatoes. Give dat to all dem dat can'
work en ain' got nobody to help dem. Dat dry milk a good
thing to mix up de bread wid en den it a help to fix little
milk en bread for dem two little ones. De potatoes, I stews
dem for de chillun too. Dey mighty fond of dem. Now de oatmeal, de chillun don' eat dat so I fixes it for Sue en every
now en den I takes a little bit wid my breakfast."

"I don' know much what to tell you bout Abraham Lincoln.
I think he was a mighty great man, a mighty great man, what I
hear of him."

"I remembers de Yankees come dere to my white folks
plantation one day en, child, dere was a time on dat place.
All dem niggers was just a kickin up dey heels en shoutin.
I was standin dere on de piazza lookin at dem en I say, 'I
don' see why dey want to carry on like dat for. I been free
all de time.' When dey get through de Yankees tell dem dey
was free as dey Massa was en give dem so many bushels of corn
en so much meat for dey own. Some take dey pile en go on off
en some choose to stay on dere wid dey Missus. She was good

Code No.
Project, 1885-(1)
Prepared by Annie Ruth Davis
Place, Marion, S.C.
Date, September 10, 1937

No. Words_____
Reduced from___words
Rewritten by
Page 3.

143

to all her colored people en dey stay on dere for part de
crop. Give dem so much of de crop accordin to de chillun
dey had to feed. I know dis much, dey all know dey gwine
get 12 bushels of corn a year, if dey ain' get no more. Dat
a bushel every month. Yes, dat how it was."

"O Lord, baby, I don' know a thing bout none of dat thing
call conjurin. Don' know nothin bout it. Dat de devil work
en I ain' bother wid it. Dey say some people can kill you,
but dey ain' bother me. Some put dey trust in it, but not
me. I put my trust in de Lord cause I know it just a talk
de people have. No, Lord, I can' remember dat neither. I
hear dem say Raw Head en Bloody Bones would catch you if you
be bad, but how it started, I don' know. I know I don' know
nothin bout how dey look en I don' want to see dem neither.
No, child, people say dey sho to be, but I ain' see none.
How dey look, I don' know."

"I don' know what to think bout de times dese days.
De times worse den dey used to be, child, You know dey worse.
Dis here a fast time de people livin on cause everybody know
de people die out heap faster den dey used to. Don' care how
dey kill you up. No, child, dey sho worser. My people en
yunnah people. Don' it seem so to you dat dey worser?"

"Baby, I got to get up from here en leave now cause I
huntin medicine dis mornin. I ain' got time to tell you
nothin else dis time, but I gwine get my mind fix up on it

Code No.
Project,1885-(1)
Prepared by Annie Ruth Davis
Place, Marion, S.C.
Date, September 10, 1937

No. Words_____
Reduced from___words
Rewritten by

Page 4.

144

en den your old black mammy comin back fore long en stay
all day wid you en your mamma. What time dat clock say
it now, honey? I got to hurry en catch de doctor fore he
get away from his office en be so scatter bout till nobody
can' tell whe' he is. Dr. Dibble a good doctor, a mighty
good doctor. When he come, don' never come in no hurry.
Takes pains wid you. Dat been my doctor. I is just devoted
to him."

Source: Mom Sara Brown, ex-slave, age 85, Marion, S.C.
         Second Report.

         Personal interview, September, 1937 by Annie Ruth
         Davis, Marion, S.C.

(Some recollections of 'The Reb Time day' given by

Aunt Margaret Bryant)

Visitor: "How are you Aunt Margaret?"

Margaret: "Missus, I ain't wuth! I ain't wuth!"

Visitor: "Aunt Margaret you've been here a long time.
How old are you?"

Margaret: "I can't tell you my age no way in the world!
When freedom come, I been here. Not big nuff (enough)
for work for the Reb, but I been here Reb time. Been
big nuff (enough) to know when Yankee gun-boat come to
Watsaw (Wachesaw). Whole gang o' Yankee come to the
house and didn't do a thing but ketch (catch) a gang o'
fowl and gone on. And tell the people (meaning the
slaves) to take the house and go in and get what they
want. The obersheer (overseer) hear the Doctor whistle
to the gate and wabe (wave) him back. And then the Doctor know the Yankee been there and he gone on to the
creek house and get all he gold and ting (thing) out
the house and gone -- Marion till Freedom then he
come back.

        "Yankee come in that night. Moon shine lak
a day. Stay in the Doctor house that night. Morning
come, take a gang o' fowl and gone on!

Visitor: "Aunt Margaret, what was your name before you
were married?"

Margaret: "Margaret One. Brother and sister? I ain't
one when I come here. Ain't meet aunty, uncle - none.
Me and my brudder Michael wuz twin. I ain't meet none
when I come here. All been sell. Me and my Ma One here.
Mary One. Husband title, husband nichel (initial) been
'One.' Number one carpenter - give 'em that name
Michael One - and he gibe 'em that name. Born Sandy
Island. Been to landing to Watsaw when gun-boat come.
Just a sneak long! Boat white. Hab (have) a red chimb-
ley (chimney.) Didn't try to carry we off. Tell 'em
'Go and help youself.' Been after the buckra. (The
Yankee trying to catch the buckra.)

      "I see my Ma dye with some bush they call 'indigo,'
and black walnut bark. Big old pen for the sheep - folds.

      "My Pa sister, Ritta One had that job. Nuss (nurse)
the chillun. Chillun house. One woman nuss (nurse) all
the chillun while they ma in the field - rice field.
All size chillun. Git the gipsy (gypsum) weed. Beat 'em
up for worm. Give 'em when the moon change. Take a buck-
et and follow dem. And tell the Doctor how much a worm
that one make and that one and count dem (them). When
the moon change, do that.

      "I have one born with caul. Loss he caul. Rat carry
'em. Ain't here; he see nothin. (The custom seems to be,

to preserve the caul.)

"Child born feet fore-most see 'um too." (See spirit)
"Talk chillun? Put duh switch. Put you 'Bull pen.' Hab
'um (have them) a place can't see you hand before you.
Can't turn round good in there. Left you in there till
morning. Give you fifty lash and send you to work. You
ain't done that task, man and woman lick!

"Couldn't manage my ma. Obersheer (overseer) want to
lick ma, Mary One say, 'Going drownded meself! I done my
work! Fore I take a lick, rather drownded meself.'"
Obersheer gone tell the Doctor. Tie her long rope. Right
to Sandy Island. Man hold the rope. Gone on. Jump in
river. So Doctor say, 'You too good labor for drown.
Take dem (them) to Watsaw.' Me and she and man what paddle
the boat. Bring her to weave. Two womans fuh card; two
spin. Ma wop 'em off. Sail duh sheckel (shuttle) through
there.

"Po- buckra come there and buy cloth from Ma. Buy three
and four yard. Ma sell that, have to weave day and night to
make up that cloth to please obersheer. Come big day time.
'Little chillun, whey (where) Mama?' Tell 'em Ma to the
weaving house. Don't have money fuh pay. Bring hog and
such like as that to pay.

"You know Marse Allard age? Me and Marse Allard suck

together. Me and Marse Allard and my brudder Michael. My
ma fadder mix wid (with) the Injun. Son Larry Aikens.
Stay Charston (Charlestown). Just as clean! (Meaning
Larry, her Uncle, very bright skin. Mixed with Indian.)
See 'em the one time. Come from Charston bring Doctor
two horse."

                    Given by Aunt Margaret Bryant
                    Age - (Born before Freedom)
                    Murrells Inlet, S. C.

SAVILLA BURRELL, EX-SLAVE 83 YEARS.

"Our preacher, Beaty, told me that you wanted to see me today. I walked three miles dis mornin' before the sun gits hot to dis house. Dis house is my grand daughter's house. Willie Caldwell, her husband, work down to de cotton mill. Him make good money and take good care of her, bless the Lord, I say."

"My Marster in slavery time was Captain Tom Still. He had big plantation down dere on Jackson Crick. My Mistress name was Mary Ann, though she wasn't his fust wife--jest a second wife, and a widow when she captivated him. You know widows is like dat anyhow, 'cause day done had 'sperience wid mens and wraps dem 'round their little finger and git dem under their thumb for the mens knows what gwine on. Young gals have a poor chance against a young widow like Miss Mary Ann was. Her had her troubles with Marse Tom after her git him, I tell you, but maybe best not to tell dat right now anyways."

"Marse Tom had four chillun by his fust wife, dey was John, Sam, Henretta and I can't 'member de name of the other one; least right now. Dey teached me to call chillun three years old, young Marse and say Missie. Dey whip you if dey ever hear you say old Marse or old Missie. Dat riled dem."

"My pappy name Sam, My mother name Mary. My pappy did not live on the same place as mother. He was a slave of de Hamiltons, and he git a pass sometimes to come and be with her; not often. Grandmammy name Ester and she belonged to our Marse Tom Still, too."

"Us lived in a log cabin wid a stick chimney. One time de sticks got afire and burnt a big hole in de back of de chimney in cold winter time wid the wind blowing, and dat house was filled wid fire-sparks, ashes, and smoke for weeks 'fore dey tore dat chimney down and built another jest like the old one. De bed was nailed to de side of de walls. How many rooms? Jest one room."

"Never seen any money. How many slaves? So many you couldn't count dem. Dere was plenty to eat sich as it was, but in the summer time before us git dere to eat de flies would be all over de food and some was swimmin' in de gravy and milk pots. Marse laugh 'bout dat, and say, it made us fat."

"Dey sell one of mother's chillun once, and when she take on and cry 'bout it, Marse say, 'stop dat sniffin' dere if you don't want to git a whippin'.' She grieve and cry at night 'bout it. Clothes? Yes Sir, Us half naked all de time. Grown boys went 'round bare footed and in dey shirt tail all de summer."

"Marse was a rich man. 'Fore Christmus dey would kill thirty hogs and after Christmus, thirty more hogs. He had a big gin house and sheep, goats, cows, mules, hosses, turkeys, geese, and a stallion; I members his name, Stockin'-Foot. Us little niggers was skeered to death of dat stallion. Mothers used to say to chillun to quiet dem, 'Better hush, Stockin'-Foot will git you and tramp you down." Any child would git quiet at dat."

"Old Marse was de daddy of some mulatto chillun. De 'lations wid the mothers of dese chillun is what give so much grief to Mistress. De neighbors would talk 'bout it and he would sell all dem chillun away from dey mothers to a trader. My Mistress would cry 'bout dat.

"Our doctor was old Marse son-in-law, Dr. Martin. I seen him cup a man once. He was a good doctor. He give slaves castor oil, bleed dem some times and make dem take pills."

"Us looked for the Yankees on dat place like us look now for de Savior and de host of angels at de second comin'. Dey come one day in February. Dey took everything carryable off de plantation and burnt de big house, stables, barns, gin house and dey left the slave houses."

"After de war I marry Osborne Burrell and live on de Tom Jordan place. I'se de mother of twelve chillun. Jest three livin' now. I lives wid the Mills family three miles 'bove town. My son Willie got killed at de DuPont Powder Plant at Hopewell, Virginia, during de World War. Dis house you settin' in belongs to Charlie Caldwell. He marry my grand daughter, Willie B. She is twenty-three years old."

"Young Marse Sam Still got killed in de Civil War. Old Marse live on. I went to see him in his last days and I set by him and kept de flies off while dere. I see the lines of sorrow had plowed on dat old face and I 'membered he'd been a captain on hoss back in dat war. It come into my 'membrance de song of Moses; 'de Lord had triumphed glorily and de hoss and his rider have been throwed into de sea'."

"You been good to listen. Dis is the fust time I can git to speak my mind like dis mornin'. All de people seem runnin' here and yonder, after dis and after dat. Dere is a nudder old slave, I'se qwine to bring him down here Saturday and talk to you again."

Project 1885-1
FOLKLORE
Spartanburg, S.C.
Sept. 15, 1937

390230

152
Edited by:
Elmer Turnage

STORIES FROM EX-SLAVES

"I works on de shares and makes a fair living on a rented farm; don't own no land. I was born in Newberry County, near de old Longshore store, about 12 miles northwest of Newberry Courthouse on de Henry Burton place. My parents belonged to Henry Burton in slavery time. He was our marster. I married Betty Burton, a nigger girl whose parents belonged to Marse Henry Burton, too.

"We had a good marster and mistress. Dey give us a good place to sleep and lots to eat. He had a big four-acre garden where he raised lots of vegetables fer his slaves. He had plenty meat, molasses and bread. We ground our corn and wheat and made our own feed.

"Marster wouldn't let anybody bother his slaves. He wouldn't 'low his overseers or de padrollers to whip 'em. He never whipped one.

"We had no school and no church; but was made to go to de white folks church and set in de gallery. When Freedom come, de niggers begin to git dere own church, and built small brush huts called 'brush harbors'.

"We didn't do work on Saturday afternoons, but went hunting and fishing den, while de women folks cleaned up around de place fer Sunday. De marster liked to hunt, and he hunted foxes which was plenty around dere den. Now dey is all gone.

"We danced and had gigs. Some played de fiddle and some made whistles from canes, having different lengths for different notes, and blowed 'em like mouth organs."

Source: C.B. Burton (79), Newberry, S.C.
        Interviewer: G.L. Summer, Newberry, S.C. (9/10/37)

GEORGE ANN BUTLER

Ex-Slave 75 Years

West of the paved highway at Garnett one may reach, after
several miles, the old Augusta Road that follows along the
Savannah River from Augusta to a landing point a little south
of Garnett. Miles from the busy highway, it passes, in quiet
majesty, between fields and woods, made rich by the river's
overflow and heavy dews. Nature has done her best in produc-
ing beautiful evergreen trees of immense size and much lux-
uriant shrubbery of many kinds. Live oaks, magnolias,
yellow slash pines, hollies, and many evergreen shrubs keep
the woods even in winter, a fascinating wilderness to hunters
and nature lovers. On this road George Ann Butler lives, and
has lived for the seventy-five years of her life.

"I was born an' raised on de Greenwood place. It belonged
to ole man Joe Bostick. He owned all dese places 'long dese
here road. He own de Bostick place back yonder; den he own
de Pipe Creek place next dat; den Oaklawn; den joinin' dat
was Greenwood. De Colcock's Elmwood was next. My Husband
was birth right here on de Pipe Creek, an' been here ever
since. He kin tell you more'n I kin. I was George Ann Curry
before I marry.

"I can't remember so much 'bout slavery time. I was
crawlin' over de floor when slavery time - dey tell me. But
atter de war, I 'members. Couldn't find no corn seed!
Couldn't find no cotton seed! Couldn't find no salt! You
knows it was hard times when dere wasn't no salt to season de

vegetables. Had to go down to de salt water an' get de water an' boil it for salt. Dat been a long way from here. Must be fifty or sixty mile! An' dey couldn't go so fast in dem days. Sufferin' been in de neighborhood atter de war pass!

"Cotton was de thing 'way back yonder. An' right 'long dis road dey'd haul it. Haul it to Cohen's Bluff! Haul it to Matthews Bluff! Haul it to Parichucla! Don't haul it dis way no more! Send de cotton to de railroad! But in dem days it was de ships dat carried it to Savannah. Cotton seem to be play out now - dey plant so much.

"I hear 'em tell 'bout de war, an' havin' to drill an' step when dey say step, an' throw up dey hands, when dey say throw up de hand. Everything had to be done jes' so! De war was sure a terrible thing."

Source: George Anne Butler, R. F. D. Garnett, S. C.

Project #-1655
Phoebe Faucette
Hampton County

Solbert (?)   See Ms. #3

ISAIAH BUTLER, EX-SLAVE 79 YEARS

"Yes, dis is Isaiah Butler, piece of him. Ain't much left
of him now. Yes, I knows all 'bout dis heah country from
way back. I was born and raised right on dis same place
here; lived here all my life 'sides from travellin' round a
little space. Dere was a rice field not far from dis house
here, where I plowed up more posts that had been used as
landmarks! Dis place was de Bostick place, and it jined to
de Thomson place, and de Thomson place to Edmund Martin's
place dat was turned over to Joe Lawton, his son-in-law.
Bill Daniel had charge of de rice field I was telling you
'bout. He was overseer, on de Daniel Blake place. Den
dere was de Maner place, de Trowell, de Kelly, and de Wallace
places. Back in dem times dey cultivated rice. Had mules
to cultivate it! But cotton and corn was what dey planted
most of all; 4,000 acres I think dey tell me was on dis place.
I know it supposed to be more than ten miles square. Nobody
know de landmarks 'cept me. When de Bostick boys came back
from out west last year, dey had to come to me to find out
where dere place was. Dey didn't know nuttin' 'bout it. Dey
used to use twenty plow, and de hoe hands was over a hundred,
I know.

"I 'member when de Yankees come through. I was no more'n
a lad, nine or ten years old. Bostick had a big ginhouse,
barn, stables, and such like. And when de soldiers come a
goat was up on de platform in front of de door to de loft of

de barn. Dere were some steps leadin' up dere and dat goat
would walk up dem steps same as any body. De fuss thing de
Yankees do, dey shoot dat goat. Den dey start and tear up
eberyt'ing. All de white folks had refugee up North, and
dey didn't do nuttin' to us niggers.

"Fore dat time I was jes' a little boy too young to do
nuttin'. Jes' played aroun' in de street. Ole Mr. Ben Bostick used to bring clothes an' shoes to us and see dat we
was well cared for. Dere was nineteen houses in de street
for us colored folks. Dey wuz all left by de soldiers. But
in de year 1882 dere come a cyclone (some folks call it a
tornado), and knocked down every house; only left four standing. Pieces of clothes and t'ings were carried for four or
five miles from here. It left our house; but it took every-
t'ing we had. It took de walls of de house, jes' left de
floorin', an' it wuz turn 'round. Took everyt'ing! I'd jes'
been married 'bout a year, and you know how dat is. We jes'
had to scuffle and scuffle 'roun' till de Lord bless us.

"Dere wuz plenty of deer, squirrel, possum, an' rabbits in
dem times; no more dan dere is now, but dere wuz no hinderance
den as now. De deer come right up to my door now; dey come
all 'roun' dis house, and we cain't do nuttin'. De other day
one wuz over dere by dat peachtree, an' not long ago four of
em come walkin' right through dis yard. I don't go fishin' no
more. Folks say de streams is all dried up. But I used to be

a good fisherman, me an' me ole woman. She's spryer'n me now.
I used to allus protect her when we wuz young, an' now its her
dat's acarin' for me. We had our gardens in de ole days, too.
Oh, yes'm. Little patches of collards, greens an' t'ings, but
now I ain't able to do nuttin', jes' hang 'roûn' de place here.

"My father used to belong to General Butler, Dennis Butler
was his name. My mother was a Maner, but originally she wuz
draw out of de Robert estate. Ole Ben Bostick fuss wife wuz a
Robert. Dey wuz sure wealthy folks. One of 'em went off to
sail. Bill F. Robert wuz his name. He had so much money dat
he say dat he goin' to de end of de world. He come back an'
he say he went so close hell de heat draw de pitch from de
vessel. But he lost his eyesight by it. Wa'n't (it was not)
long after he got back dat he went stone blind.

"My ole boss, preacher Joe Bostick wuz one of de best of men.
He wuz hard of hearin' like I is, an' a good ole man. But de
ole lady, ole "Miss Jenny", she wuz very rough. She hired all
de overseers, and she do all. If'n anybody try to go to de
old man wid anyt'ing, she'd talk to 'em herself an' not let 'em
see de old man.

"In slavery time de slaves wuz waked up every morning byd de
colored over-driver blowin' a horn. Ole man Jake Chisolm wuz
his name. Jes' at daybreak, he'd put his horn through a crack
in de upper part of de wall to his house an' blow it through
dat crack. Den de under-driver would go out an' round 'em up.

When dey done all dey day-work, dey come home an' cook dey supper,
an' wash up. Den dey blow de horn for 'em to go to bed. Sometime
dey have to out de fire an' finish dey supper in de dark. De
under-driver, he'd go out den and see who ain't go to bed. He
wouldn't say anyt'ing den; but next mornin' he'd report it to de
overseer, an' dem as hadn't gone to bed would be whipped.

"My mother used to tell me dat if any didn't do dey day's work,
dey'd be put in de stocks or de bill-bo. You know each wuz
given a certain task dat had to be finish dat day. Dat what dey
call de day-work. When dey put 'em in de stocks dey tie 'em hand
and foot to a stick. Dey could lie down wid dat. I hear of
colored folks doin' dat now to dere chillun when dey don't do.
Now de bill-bo wuz a stabe (stave) drove in de ground, an' dey
tied dere hands and den dere feet to dat, standin' up. Dey'd
work on Saturday but dey wuz give Sundays. Rations wuz give out
on Mondays. Edmund Lawton went over to Louisiana to work on de
Catherine Goride place, but he come back, 'cause he say dey blow
dey horn for work on Sunday same as any other day, and he say he
wa'n't goin' to work on no Sunday. Dey didn't have a jail in dem
times. Dey'd whip 'em, and dey'd sell 'em. Every slave know
what, 'I'll put you in my pocket, sir!' mean.

"De slaves would walk when dey'd go anywhere. If'n dey buy a
bunch of slaves in New Orleans, dey'd walk by night and day. I
'member when one young girl come back from refugin' wid de white
folks, her feet were jes' ready to buss open, and dat wuz all.

You couldn't travel unless de boss give you a pass. De Ku Klan
had "patrol" all about in de bushes by de side of de road at
night. And when dey caught you dey'd whip you almost to death!
Dey'd horsewhip you. Dey didn't run away nowhere 'cause dey
knowed dey couldn't.

"If'n you wanted to send any news to anybody on another plantation, de overseer'd write de message for you and send it by a
boy to de overseer of de other plantation, and he'd read it to
de one you wrote to.

"When de war wuz over, ole man Jones come over frum Georgia
and sell t'ings to de colored folks. He'd sell 'em everyt'ing.
He took all de colored folks' money!

"I learned to read when I wuz goin' to school when I wuz
about fifteen years old, but I learned most I know after I wuz
married, at night school, over on de Morrison place. De colored folks had de school, but 'course Mr. Morrison was delighted
to know dey wuz havin' it. As for church, in de olden times,
people used to, more or less, attend under de bush-arbor. In
1875 when I jined de church, ole man John Butler wuz de preacher.

"Ghosts? I'se met plenty of um! When I wuz courtin' I met
many a one - One got me in de water, once. And another time
when I wuz crossing a stream, I wuz on de butt end of de log,
an' dey wuz on de blossom end, an' we meet jes' as close as I
is to you now. I say to him, same as to anybody, 'I sure ain't

goin' to turn back and fall off dis log. Now de best t'ing
for you to do is to turn 'round and let me come atter (after)
you. You jes' got to talk to 'em same as to anybody. It
don't pay to be 'fraid of 'em. So he wheel 'round. (Spirits
can wheel, you know.) And when he get to de end of de log,
I say, 'Now you off and I off. You kin go on 'cross now.'
Dey sure is a t'ing, all right! Dey look jes' like anybody
else, 'cept'n it's jes' cloudy and misty like it goin' to
pour down rain. But it don't do to be 'fraid of 'em. I
ain't 'fraid of nuttin', myself. I never see 'em no more.
Guess I jes' sorta out-growed 'em. But dere sure is sech a
t'ing, all right! De white folks'd see 'em, too. I 'member
hearin' ole Joe Bostick, de preacher, say to a man, by de
name of Tinlin, 'Did you hear dat hog barkin' last night?
Well, de spirit come right in de house. Come right up over
de mantlepiece.' (It) wuz in de field workin' same as I allus | I (?)
done, and I hear'd ole Joe horse a snortin'. Ole Joe didn't
want nuttin'. He jes' want to see what I wuz doin'.

"Abraham Lincoln done all he could for de colored folks.
But dey cain't none of 'em do nuttin' without de Lord."
Source: Isaiah Butler, Garnett, S. C.

TITLES IN THE

SLAVE NARRATIVES SERIES

FROM APPLEWOOD BOOKS

ALABAMA SLAVE NARRATIVES
ISBN 1-55709-010-6 • $14.95
Paperback • 7-1/2" x 9-1/4" • 168 pp

ARKANSAS SLAVE NARRATIVES
ISBN 1-55709-011-4 • $14.95
Paperback • 7-1/2" x 9-1/4" • 172 pp

FLORIDA SLAVE NARRATIVES
ISBN 1-55709-012-2 • $14.95
Paperback • 7-1/2" x 9-1/4" • 168 pp

GEORGIA SLAVE NARRATIVES
ISBN 1-55709-013-0 • $14.95
Paperback • 7-1/2" x 9-1/4" • 172 pp

INDIANA SLAVE NARRATIVES
ISBN 1-55709-014-9 • $14.95
Paperback • 7-1/2" x 9-1/4" • 140 pp

KENTUCKY SLAVE NARRATIVES
ISBN 1-55709-016-5 • $14.95
Paperback • 7-1/2" x 9-1/4" • 136 pp

MARYLAND SLAVE NARRATIVES
ISBN 1-55709-017-3 • $14.95
Paperback • 7-1/2" x 9-1/4" • 88 pp

MISSISSIPPI SLAVE NARRATIVES
ISBN 1-55709-018-1 • $14.95
Paperback • 7-1/2" x 9-1/4" • 184 pp

MISSOURI SLAVE NARRATIVES
ISBN 1-55709-019-X • $14.95
Paperback • 7-1/2" x 9-1/4" • 172 pp

NORTH CAROLINA SLAVE NARRATIVES
ISBN 1-55709-020-3 • $14.95
Paperback • 7-1/2" x 9-1/4" • 168 pp

OHIO SLAVE NARRATIVES
ISBN 1-55709-021-1 • $14.95
Paperback • 7-1/2" x 9-1/4" • 128 pp

OKLAHOMA SLAVE NARRATIVES
ISBN 1-55709-022-X • $14.95
Paperback • 7-1/2" x 9-1/4" • 172 pp

SOUTH CAROLINA SLAVE NARRATIVES
1-55709-023-8 • $14.95
Paperback • 7-1/2" x 9-1/4" • 172 pp

TENNESSEE SLAVE NARRATIVES
ISBN 1-55709-024-6 • $14.95
Paperback • 7-1/2" x 9-1/4" • 92 pp

VIRGINIA SLAVE NARRATIVES
ISBN 1-55709-025-4 • $14.95
Paperback • 7-1/2" x 9-1/4" • 68 pp

* * * * * * * * * * * * * * *

IN THEIR VOICES: SLAVE NARRATIVES
A companion CD of original recordings
made by the Federal Writers' Project.
Former slaves from many states tell
stories, sing long-remembered songs,
and recall the era of American slavery.
This invaluable treasure trove of oral
history, through the power of voices of
those now gone, brings back to life the
people who lived in slavery.
ISBN 1-55709-026-2 • $19.95
Audio CD

* * * * * * * * * * * * * * *

TO ORDER, CALL 800-277-5312 OR
VISIT US ON THE WEB AT WWW.AWB.COM